"I wo___
if you w___ ___ ___ key.

Jerralee's eyes narrowed suspiciously.

"Why in heaven's name would I do that?" Nic asked innocently.

"To keep me here against my will," she said brazenly.

"Lady, you have been sorely misled if you think I have to lock women in the attic to hold their interest."

"Maybe not other women," she replied, refusing to back down.

"Not you, either." He caressed her cheek with one hand and drew his thumb back and forth over the lips that taunted him. His other hand grasped her waist and pulled her against him.

Willfully, his mouth lowered to hers, and Jerralee made no move to stop him.

What followed was the sweetest, most devastating kiss she had ever had. It was a rollercoaster ride of a kiss. An earthquake of a kiss. A kiss fated to alter reality and change the course of human events.

It was, in a word... magic.

Dear Reader,

At Silhouette Romance we're starting the New Year off right! This month we're proud to present *Donavan*, the ninth wonderful book in Diana Palmer's enormously popular LONG, TALL TEXANS series. *The Taming of the Teen* is a delightful sequel to Marie Ferrarella's *Man Trouble*—and Marie promises that Angelo's story is coming soon. Maggi Charles returns with the tantalizing *Keep It Private* and Jody McCrae makes her debut with the charming *Lake of Dreams*. Pepper Adams's *That Old Black Magic* casts a spell of love in the Louisiana bayou—but watch out for Crevi the crocodile!

Of course, no lineup in 1992 would be complete without our special WRITTEN IN THE STARS selection. This month we're featuring the courtly Capricorn man in Joan Smith's *For Richer, for Poorer*.

Throughout the year we'll be publishing stories of love by all of your favorite Silhouette Romance authors—Diana Palmer, Brittany Young, Annette Broadrick, Suzanne Carey and many, many more. The Silhouette Romance authors and editors love to hear from readers, and we'd love to hear from *you!*

Happy New Year...and happy reading!

Valerie Susan Hayward
Senior Editor

PEPPER ADAMS

That Old
Black Magic

Silhouette ❤ *Romance*

Published by Silhouette Books New York
America's Publisher of Contemporary Romance

We would like to dedicate this book to everyone who
believes in magic and to those who believe in love.
But then, what is one without the other?

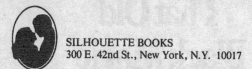

SILHOUETTE BOOKS
300 E. 42nd St., New York, N.Y. 10017

THAT OLD BLACK MAGIC

ISBN: 0-373-08842-6

First Silhouette Books printing January 1992

All the characters in this book have no existence
outside the imagination of the author and have
no relation whatsoever to anyone bearing the same
name or names. They are not even distantly
inspired by any individual known or unknown
to the author, and all incidents are pure invention.

Printed in the U.S.A.

PEPPER ADAMS

lives in Oklahoma with her husband and children. Her interest in romance writing began with obsessive reading and was followed by writing courses, where she learned the craft. She longs for the discipline of the "rigid schedule" all the how-to books exhort writers to maintain, but does not seriously believe she will achieve one in this lifetime. She finds she works best if she remembers to take her writing, and not herself, seriously.

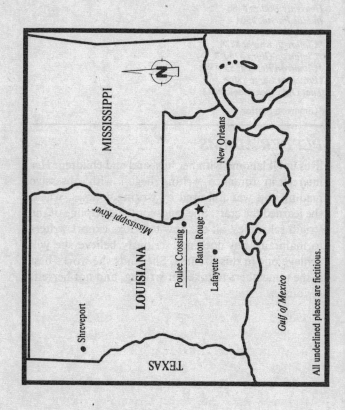

All underlined places are fictitious.

Chapter One

"I simply am not interested in trying to reverse the hex." The infamous family curse was the last thing Nic Delarue wanted to discuss over dinner, but seeing Zareh's horrified expression, he softened his words with a smile.

The woman had cared for him since birth, and even though her official role was now that of housekeeper, Zareh Dulac meant much more to him than the title implied. She was a good friend and, since his father's death, the closest thing he had to family. Their long association made them tolerant of each other's eccentricities.

Living with Zareh often required a great deal of tolerance—especially when it came to voodoo. Not only did she believe in it, she practiced it. Of course, her version did not include dark rituals of chicken blood and sacrifice. Rather, she followed the innocuous folkways of her African ancestors to create potions, charms and entrancements for the benefit of others. She reputedly had the power to get rid of warts, bring home errant husbands and predict the sex of unborn children, among other things. Hers was a natural magic used for good, never evil.

Still, living with someone bent on solving everyday problems through supernatural means could be trying at times.

"Not interested?" The tall, dark-skinned woman set a fragrant dish of crawfish pie in front of him. "M'sieu Nic, you wish to have a family, *non?*" Like others along the bayou, her speech was a unique and musical blend of both French and English.

"I would like nothing better. But I fear my judgment is a bit faulty when it comes to women."

Zareh responded to the reference to his former marriage with an eloquent shrug. "You did not choose that one, she chose you. She was too young, too obsessed with money, and she come from New Orleans. *Sacré!*"

Zareh had always held Justine's background accountable for her flaws. Perhaps she was right to do so. His ex-wife was the pampered daughter of a wealthy New Orleans cottonbroker, and was accustomed to a dizzying social life. She couldn't adjust to the slower pace of Poulee Crossing, and had found his hometown provincial and totally lacking in charm. After four stormy years they had reached an impasse.

He refused to leave, and she refused to stay. He'd found solace in his work, and she'd run home to Daddy.

"I tell you this before, *non?*" An airy wave of her arm brought Zareh's many silver bracelets jingling to life.

"Yes," Nic agreed with a wry smile. "Many, many times."

"Then when you almos' make another marriage, did I not warn you about that Bettina woman?"

Nic's eyes narrowed as he recalled his marital near miss. Bettina would have hated Poulee Crossing as much as Justine had. Fortunately, by breaking their engagement to elope with an orthodontist from Baton Rouge, Bettina had saved them both a great deal of trouble.

"You could say that. You refused to speak to me for a week after I announced our engagement. As I recall, you never did speak to her."

"Lucky she run off with that toothman, or mebbe I still not be speak' to you," Zareh retorted with a toss of her silk-wrapped head.

Hoping to end the conversation, Nic turned his attention to his crawfish pie.

Zareh, however, was not so easily sidetracked. "You must listen to old Zareh and do as she say nex' time." She was over sixty, but her café au lait skin was smooth and unwrinkled. Her raisin-dark eyes were bright with impossible youth, her teeth even and white and perfect. Her well-preserved appearance was almost enough to make Nic believe in all those outlandish charms of hers.

"I don't want to try again," he insisted.

"You mus' have an heir! You are the last of the Delarues. You mus' not give up looking for a wife."

Resolutely, she folded her arms across her ample bosom. "If you do, poor Zareh will be force' to help."

The prospect of Zareh's kind of help made Nic put down his fork. He said firmly, "You've taken good care of me all my life, and I love you like a mother. But there is a limit to how much I will allow you to meddle in my affairs."

"Affairs, hah! Enough of affairs. You must marry and your wife must conceive before your next birthday or the Delarue line will be 'poof!' Not'ing. That much I know for a sure fact."

A spark of interest lit up Nic's dark eyes. "That's the first I've heard of an age limit on the curse."

"I have look' into it," Zareh informed him. "Since Jules LeBeau order' the curse, no Delarue mens have fathered children after age thirty-five." She pointed a long finger at him. "Your time, she is running out."

Nic sighed. "How many times do I have to tell you? I do not believe in curses or spells or voodoo magic. As far as heirs go, my virility has been medically documented, and no curse can change that."

For years Zareh had been so preoccupied with the fate of the Delarues that her worries had finally affected his own good sense in the matter, and he had resorted to fertility testing to allay the doubts she'd raised.

"*Docteurs!* They don' know everyt'ing. That first wife, she not get with child."

"Justine and I never tried to have a child, she was too immature herself." Hoping she'd let the matter drop, he added, "We took precautions."

"Aha!" Zareh exclaimed. "So that is why my *bébé* potion did not work."

"You and your infernal potions," he muttered. "They are the bane of my existence."

"Do not let the past trouble you, M'sieu Nic. I have finally learn' how to reverse the spell and end the curse for all time." Zareh's white teeth flashed in a satisfied smile. "After all, my *p'père*, old Belzac, was the conjurer Jules LeBeau hire' to place the curse on your fam'ly."

"I know all that. But as I've told you, I don't care. I still don't believe in such things."

"Yes, yes," she said impatiently. "But you will listen allasame."

"No. I have put up with chicken feathers under my pillow and with my own personal juju hanging over my bedroom door. Enough is enough. I have to draw the line somewhere."

"But never do I ask for much, M'sieu Nic," she said, pouting. "Only that you listen to old Zareh." Her regal chin dropped, and she cast her dark eyes down toward her bare feet. She hated shoes, and wore them only when there were guests in the house. "Can you not do that little bit for a poor old woman who cares for you?"

There was nothing poor or old about Zareh Dulac, but Nic knew better than to argue. Whether he believed in her magic or not, his old friend had been blessed with a powerful personality. "All right. I'll hear you out, but I will not participate in any mumbo jumbo."

Her face brightened, and she was happy again. "As I have tol' you, I speak to many two-headed *docteurs* t'ru the years, and I now know what mus' be done. Soon I will conjure another spell to reverse Belzac's."

"That's nice, Zareh." Nothing else had worked to end the discussion, he would try indulgence. More interested in satisfying his hunger than his curiosity, Nic tasted the savory dish before him.

"And very soon you will be married."

"Really?" A dark eyebrow quirked in sardonic amusement. "In that case, perhaps you should press my best suit."

The tall woman gathered herself up proudly. "*C'est* okay you make fun. I will be the one laugh' when you make a marriage."

"What are you going to do?" he asked suspiciously. Even if he didn't believe in voodoo, he had a healthy respect for the practice and was wary of Zareh's intentions.

"Don' you worry, *chérie*. You won't even know when it be happen'."

He didn't like the sound of that. "Pray tell me what is required to end the notorious curse."

"*Certainement. C'est simple.* All you mus' do is marry a LeBeau." Zareh delivered that bombshell with consummate relish.

Nic laughed, and nearly choked on crawfish pie. The LeBeaus and Delarues had been feuding for years. The two families barely spoke to each other, much less intermarried.

"Is that all?" he asked with an exaggerated sigh of relief. "I was worried I might have to do something difficult like swallow a live chicken."

Zareh arched her perfect ebony eyebrows and ignored his sarcasm. No matter how absurd her "cure" sounded, she was obviously serious about it.

Nic composed himself enough to probe further. "There are more LeBeaus in this parish then musk-rats in the swamp. Do you mind telling me which of the lovely LeBeau ladies is to be my bride?"

"*Certainement.* In a few weeks only, you will marry—" Zareh paused for dramatic effect "—Mam'selle Jerralee LeBeau."

Nic's laughter died suddenly and he stared at Zareh in astonishment. Jerralee LeBeau? Impossible. Of the dozens of LeBeaus, none were so militant in their ob-servance of the ancient feud as she was.

Independent and unconventional, Jerralee flouted local custom by refusing to settle down to marriage. Instead, she ran an electrical repair business in Poulee Crossing, a most unwomanly occupation according to local opinion. As if that were not proof enough of her maverick streak, it was also rumored that she kept a pet alligator.

Since LeBeaus did not socialize with Delarues and she refused to do business with him, Nic had never actually met the woman. But as was common in small towns, he knew almost everything about her.

When her father Tiboy LeBeau had died, she had inherited the Sweetwood plantation house, property that Nic himself had been trying to purchase for years. He still made regular offers for the place through Jer-ralee's attorney-cousin, but she regularly and stub-bornly refused to sell.

For the last hundred years the Sweetwood house had been surrounded by Delarue land, so the *maison* was as worthless to her as it had been to her father and its previous owners. But just like them, Jerralee was too hardheaded to accept a reasonable offer.

"So?" Zareh asked brightly. "What you t'ink, M'sieu Nic?"

"I think you need to take another look at those chicken bones of yours, Zareh. I wouldn't marry that woman if I had malaria and she was the only cure."

"Love is very strong medicine," Zareh replied cryptically.

"Love?" There was a lot of bitterness in the short word. "I assure you, there is no love lost between Jerralee LeBeau and myself. Only yesterday she crossed the street so that she wouldn't have to pass too close to me." Jerralee's scorn disturbed him more than pride would allow him to admit, especially since he knew that he had done nothing to warrant it.

"That is not'ing," Zareh harrumphed.

"Only total indifference. If I were foolish enough to ask that little wildcat to marry me—which I am not— she would no doubt challenge me to a duel for the insult."

"She is a good, old-fashioned Acadian girl. She respects tradition, that is all. She will change. All them Acadians marry young. She mus' make a marriage soon."

"Not with me, she doesn't." Nic picked at his now-cold food. The mere idea of his marrying Jerralee LeBeau was too ridiculous for further comment.

"Her people worry that she will be an old maid."

"And well they should. I doubt there's a man in the parish who would tolerate her for very long."

His vehemence made Zareh smile. "I don' think them LeBeaus care much who the groom is, just so there is one."

"Whoever he is, he has my deepest sympathy."

"You mus' marry her, M'sieu Nic," Zareh persisted. "To remove the curse."

"I'll take the curse anytime. Besides, the woman hates me."

Zareh shrugged. "Mebbe for now. But she does not know you so good, I t'ink. You are handsome and charming, M'sieu Nic. You could change her mind, if you tried."

"I could also wrestle alligators if I tried," he scoffed. "Either enterprise would be equally hazardous." As beautiful as she was, Jerralee was also infuriatingly headstrong and her stubbornness was legendary. Without ever having spoken to him, she had made him her enemy because of an alleged wrong his ancestors had done hers years before.

Her behavior would seem ludicrous to strangers, but knowing the ways of the local people, Nic could almost understand it. His own father had never had a kind word for the LeBeaus. Bayou families were fiercely loyal to one another. Good neighborliness was common and excessive and they were always willing to offer friends a helping hand. But when a wrong was perceived, whether real or imagined, sharp feuds could develop. Resentment often flared long after the reason for the quarrel had been forgotten. What started as mutual enmity sometimes even became legend, as it had between the LeBeaus and Delarues.

"You are the first Delarue willing to forget the feud," Zareh reminded him. "Are not a few of the LeBeaus also willing?"

"A few," he conceded. "But their number does not include Jerralee." Acknowledging that fact was difficult, so he added with forced disdain, "What makes you think I would want her? She's arrogant beyond words, impossibly stubborn and spiteful enough to hold a grudge that should have been forgotten years ago. Some wife she would make.''

"No worry. I jes' give her a potion and—''

"No! That you will not do." Nic forced his voice down to a calmer level. "Stay out of it, Zareh.''

"But then the Delarue line will end with you, and I promise' your mother before she die that I would take good care of you.''

"And you have, for over thirty years. But I'm a grown man now, and I can take care of myself.''

Zareh could be relentless. "I know you. You cannot be happy wit'out a wife and many *bébés.* ''

"I'll muddle through somehow." Nic did not seriously believe in her superstitious magic, but just to be on the safe side, he emphasized, "You are not to give anyone any potion of any kind. Do I have your word on that?''

Zareh's chin rose petulantly. "Very well.''

Just so there would be no misunderstandings, he repeated, "No potions?''

"No potions.''

"Good. I'm glad we agree.''

"But when Mam'selle LeBeau come' to you, you will please try to woo her, yes?''

"No!" Nic almost told Zareh how his previous attempts to approach Jerralee had been rebuffed, but again pride prevented the revelation. "She'll never come to Long Shadows. She avoids this place like a graveyard at midnight.''

Zareh's mysterious smile was that of a satisfied cat. "She will come. These t'ings I know.''

"I don't like that sphinxlike look. Have you been rattling those chicken bones again?"

"I have done not'ing," she insisted. "But the LeBeau woman appeals to you, does she not?"

Jerralee LeBeau. Just the thought of her made a reluctant smile crease Nic's handsome features. As incorrigible as she was, she was also beautiful in an earthy, untamed way. She was no more than five foot two, but her body was lush and curvy. Her blond hair and damnably blue eyes contrasted exotically with her olive complexion. She was an intriguing woman in more ways than one. That quality, and the fact that she held Nic in such low regard, exasperated him more than anything else about her.

"Yes," he confessed. "God help me, but she does."

Chapter Two

Jerralee LeBeau stood in the middle of her aunt's crowded kitchen and clutched the treasured piece of parchment tightly in her hand. "This is it, Tante Olivette. This little old paper is the answer to all our prayers."

Always busy no matter what the occasion, the older woman looked up from the pan of shrimp she was cleaning and frowned. "That only be a scrap of old paper, *chér.* It might be the answer to *my* prayers if it was your marriage license."

Cousin Beatrix, who was Jerralee's *cousin second-aire,* nodded solemnly. "Poor Tante Olivette, I know how you feel. My Odile is twenty-five and unmarried."

Olivette's knife worked over the shellfish efficiently. "But Odile is a man, and men can wait as long as they want to speak their vows. Women cannot."

Jerralee plopped down in a chair. Since the death of her parents, two years apart, Tante Olivette and Nonc Albert had assumed the role of guardians. It didn't seem to matter to them that she was a grown woman, twenty-six years old and perfectly capable of caring for herself, of deciding when and whom she would marry.

"Things are different today," she told the two older women. Not that she hadn't often pointed out how antiquated their views on marriage were. "Women have more options. We don't have to get married anymore."

"You do in this fam'ly," Tante Olivette retorted, and was noisily seconded by the other assembled relatives.

Arguing was pointless, so Jerralee changed the subject. "We have more important matters to discuss."

Portly cousin Hercule was the only lawyer in the family, as well as the only one in town. He called for order by pounding the table with a wooden meat mallet much as a judge would pound a gavel.

"Jerralee's right. We called this family meeting to talk about the craft guild, and since I haven't had my supper yet, I say we get back to that subject."

For the first time in her life Jerralee was grateful that Hercule cared more about eating than about her marital status. "Do you think we'll have trouble getting Nic Delarue to honor this old IOU?"

"Sure as there's flies on cow flop." The remark came from Richard Roubideaux, Jerralee's neglected date for the evening. His patience had apparently worn thin and he was no longer amused by the proceedings.

Hercule frowned at the young man. "We let you stay because we don' want to run off any of Jerralee's callers. But you are not family, and you have no say in these proceedings. If you don' keep quiet, I will ask you to dispose yourself to the gallery."

"Forgive me." Richard was properly contrite in the face of such floridly expressed authority.

Jerralee scowled at her cousin and led her date outside. "Richard, this matter is very important to my family."

"Yes, yes but how long you going to be? I've been waiting almos' an hour." He checked his watch. "Your Tante Olivette said pick you up at seven, and it's almos' eight o'clock."

Jerralee wasn't happy that her relatives constantly manipulated her social life, but their interference was well-intentioned enough. Aside from the general lack of money they were all experiencing, her looming spinsterhood was their favorite worry. She put up with it because she loved them.

"If you want to make a date with me in the future, Richard, call *me*," she told the young man gently. "Don't go through Tante Olivette. Now I must get back to the meeting."

"You LeBeaus are the meetin'est family I ever saw," he complained.

Jerralee smiled and shrugged. Before she could escape into the house, he called out, "How about next Saturday night?"

"What about Saturday night?" Her mind was still distracted by the long-lost IOU.

"I'll take you to the movies. *C'est* okay?"

"No," she responded with a groan. "I have plans."
Or rather Tante Olivette had plans for her. She had
arranged a date for Jerralee with yet another passably
attractive but totally uninteresting young man. Surely
the day would come when the LeBeau matchmakers
would exhaust the local supply of marriageable men.
Maybe then she would regain some control over her
life.

"Where did Richard take himself?" Tante Olivette
demanded when Jerralee slipped back into the house.

"Home, I guess."

"*Sacré,* Jerralee." Tante Olivette pronounced her
name to rhyme with Shirley, with the emphasis on the
last syllable. "I had to go to the gas station twice in
succession to prime that boy enough to call. And you
just sent him on his way?" She turned to Beatrix with
a martyr's look. "No burden is greater than ungrate-
ful children—"

Hercule cleared his throat and cut his aunt off in
midsentence with more mallet pounding.

This awakened Nonc Caesar, who worked as night
watchman at the Delarue Sugar Mill. The old man had
gotten up early to come to the meeting because no
LeBeau would ever consider missing one. As an elder
family member, his opinions were valued and re-
spected. "Could we pass on, please? I have to get myself to work by ten."

"And I still haven't had my supper," Hercule
grumbled.

"Hercule, what are our chances of getting Nic Delarue to make good on this old IOU?" Jerralee asked
again.

"Legally speakin', I'd say slim and none. Delarue is a shrewd businessman, and he's not about to fork over no eighteen thousand dollars without a fight."

"Then we'll take him to court." Jerralee wasn't as confident about that suggestion as she sounded.

"We?" Caesar exclaimed. "Don't be includ' me in any lawsuits against M'sieu Nic. I work for him, and so do all my boys."

"I'm with Caesar," Beatrix added quickly. "I'm still paying for Elodie's braces, and I need my job."

"But we're family," Jerralee argued. "And the family sticks together."

"The trouble with this family is that nearly all its members work for Delarue Sugar," Hercule pointed out.

"That's exactly why it's so important to get a craft guild started," Jerralee exclaimed. "It will give us all independence from Delarue."

"Delarue Sugar has not been so bad to us," reminded a cousin.

As much as she hated to admit it, Jerralee knew that was true. If not for the sugar mill, many people along the bayou would be out of work. "But we're LeBeaus," she said as though that were objection enough. "It goes against nature for us to be dependent on a Delarue."

"What makes you think M'sieu Nic should pay, Minette?" Nonc Albert asked, using Jerralee's ti'name, or family nickname, which was French for kitten.

"This IOU is made out to great-great-grandfather Alcee LeBeau, and it's signed by Nic's great-great-grandfather Theodule. Theodule went off and got himself killed in the Civil War before he could repay it." Her tone implied that it was just like a Delarue to try and escape an obligation by dying.

"Alcee must have put the IOU away for propriety's sake when Theodule died," she continued.

"How come nobody don' know about this IOU before now?" Nonc Caesar's wife Zu asked.

"I'm not sure," admitted Jerralee. "Maybe Alcee didn't tell the family about it. Or maybe he forgot."

That generated a hearty round of laughter. "Since when did you ever hear of a LeBeau jus' forgettin' about eighteen thousand dollars?" Nonc Caesar teased.

"Alcee LeBeau was rich then," Jerralee reminded him. "He didn't lose his fortune until the war. Maybe after he died, the family was too busy surviving to bother looking through his papers. Then the bad blood between Jules LeBeau and Antoine Delarue came up, and then there was the curse...maybe it was just plain forgotten until now."

"That's a lot of maybes," observed Nonc Albert sagely.

"But the point is, the IOU was never paid. Legally, Delarue still owes us. We can use the money to get the craft guild started."

Jerralee had been unable to believe her good luck when she'd found the document in an old trunk in the attic upstairs. She'd looked through the papers a dozen times while planning the Sweetwood Manor restoration, but had somehow overlooked the important document. On the day of her discovery, it was as though fate had led her to a new fortune. She considered it serendipity, but she was having a hard time convincing the others of that.

"Maybe M'sieu Nic think that happen a long time ago. Maybe he won't want to pay, and we cannot risk our jobs," another cousin replied. "The flyswatter factory is failing, and there aren't so many places to work on this bayou."

Hercule nodded. "Ti' Dan is right. I wouldn't count on Delarue being too agreeable."

"Surely there's no need to sue the man." Tante Olivette obviously had a plan. "Minette, you call him up and explain what you found in those old papers. M'sieu Nic is a man of honor. He will do the right t'ing."

"That's a good idea," Caesar said enthusiastically, and the others voiced their agreement.

Jerralee had her doubts. "Delarues aren't exactly famous for their honesty, you know. If it hadn't been for Antoine Delarue's cheating, we wouldn't have lost Sweetwood in the first place."

"Maybe not on that night or to that man, but it maybe been lost anyway." Tante Olivette lowered her voice out of respect for the long-dead relative. "Ever'body knows Jules was a drinker and a gambler. Antoine just took advantage of a bad combination."

"Seems to me old Jules got his revenge when he hired a conjurer to curse the Delarues," Nonc Albert added. "Folks say Nic Delarue will be the last of his line, that he will have no heirs. That's a sad t'ing." To Albert, as to all Acadian men, being deprived of a large and loving family was a fate worse than death.

"I say we give M'sieu Nic a chance," Caesar put in.

A round of aye votes greeted that proposal, and as owner of Sweetwood, Jerralee was elected official spokeswoman for the family. She sighed as she picked up the telephone.

·The last thing she wanted to do was arrange a face-to-face confrontation with Nic Delarue. She made one more effort to change her family's mind, but when that didn't work she looked up the number and dialed resignedly. Only a fool wouldn't know when she was outnumbered and outmaneuvered.

So, with the family crowding around, she made the phone call and explained the IOU. It came as no surprise to Jerralee when Delarue was unbelievably curt and advised her to take the matter up with his attorney. Obviously, the beneficent M'sieu Nic could not be bothered to deal with a mere LeBeau.

She hung up, but his aloofness only made her more determined to have it out with him. Once the meeting was over and she was alone, she called back. His housekeeper told her that M'sieu Nic was "sadly indisposed." Yeah, right, Jerralee fumed. She'd show him indisposed. In person.

The next day was Saturday. It was unlikely that Delarue would be at the mill, so Jerralee decided to go to his ancestral home, Long Shadows, uninvited and unannounced. Her anger, which had simmered all night, was very close to the boiling point as she parked her truck in the big circular driveway and strode resolutely across the vast green manicured lawn.

When no one answered her knock, she marched around to the back, not once considering that such behavior might overstep the bounds of good manners. Her boldness paid off when she discovered Delarue lounging beside a shimmering blue swimming pool.

She planned to announce her presence immediately. But the sight of him in his scrap-of-black-nylon swimsuit almost made her lose her sense of purpose. A strange feeling, warm and weakening, overcame her, and she stepped behind a large chinaberry tree to recover her composure.

The unfamiliar sensation was fleeting but disturbing, and she rationalized that, while it was unlike her to lurk about as if she were a Peeping Tom, it was wise to size up the enemy before charging into his camp.

And size him up she did. Nic Delarue was undoubtedly the most virile-looking man in the parish. However, if the curse were to be believed, he was anything but. As she watched him soak up the late-afternoon rays, the strange feeling came back, and Jerralee was appalled when she finally recognized it for what it was. Longing.

It was almost as if she was attracted to the man. But that was ridiculous. What she was experiencing could not possibly be desire. The man was her sworn enemy. And not just because of the feud, either. She had a personal reason to resent—and resist—Nic Delarue.

Rich, educated and privileged, Nic Delarue had always gotten everything he'd wanted. He'd never been thwarted by anything or anyone—except for the stubborn LeBeaus, of course. Jerralee meant to uphold family tradition.

In her opinion, Delarue wasn't satisfied that a good portion of his fortune came from land that had once rightfully belonged to the LeBeaus. He wanted Sweetwood Manor, too. He had no wish to restore it to its former opulence, as he had Long Shadows' *grande maison*. He meant to destroy Sweetwood for profit. Like other greedy Delarues before him, he wanted to tear down the beautiful old house, plow up the once-elegant but overgrown gardens and plant more sugar.

Over her dead body. Jerralee had her own plans for Sweetwood, and Nic Delarue would never get his hands on it as long as she had anything to say about it. It was her dream to restore the mansion and open it to the public, to create a center for handcrafts that featured native cuisine and live entertainment.

She also planned to use part of it to actually house a craft guild where local artisans could meet to make and market their timeless crafts. Poulee Crossing was close enough to the interstate highway to attract travelers on their way to Baton Rouge and New Orleans. Tourist dollars would be a boon to the local economy.

It would also enable some of the citizens of Poulee Crossing, many of whom were related to her one way or another, to be a little less dependent on Delarue money for their livelihoods.

Her gaze returned to Nic. He was stretched out languidly on a chaise lounge, arms dangling loosely at his sides, legs parted to catch the sun's rays. It disturbed her that his sultry pose only enhanced his aristocratic good looks. As if the lean, tautly muscled physique, the coin-perfect features, the thick dark hair and the remarkable mahogany-colored eyes needed enhancing. And, as if he had not already been favored enough by fate, he also oozed incredible masculinity and sexuality.

When Jerralee realized she was condemning the man for being attractive, she chided herself. It wasn't like her to be so enraptured by a mere handsome physique. Especially when it belonged to a man like Nic Delarue. Over the years she had resisted the charms of every male in the parish between the ages of twenty-one and fifty. She would resist his.

"It has been said that M'sieu Nic resembles a Greek god, but I t'ink he mus' look much like his valiant Norman ancestors. *Non?*"

Jerralee whirled around, and was startled to find Zareh Dulac, Nic's housekeeper, standing behind her. The six-foot-plus woman was exotically dressed in a flowing burgundy-colored burnoose. Her large feet were bare, but the many bangles adorning her arms should have announced her arrival. From her lofty height she silently appraised Jerralee.

"I'm not a trespasser," Jerralee hurried to explain. "I've come to speak to Mr. Delarue about an important matter."

Zareh waved her hand. "I know this. It is strong magic that brings lovers together." She smiled smugly. "I am very proud of my powers, even though I cannot claim to make strong medicine like Kitty Brown and Marie Leveau. But it is strong allasame, *non?*"

Her confession left Jerralee momentarily speechless. Zareh Dulac was well-known along the bayou. The locals often sought her help in matters requiring supernatural intervention.

Zareh spoke conversationally. "My own *m'mère* had the power. She was there when the Delarue curse began. Old Antoine wouldn't have been harmed if not for his weakness for *cigares*. Your *great-grandpère* sent them to him with the deed for the Sweetwood land. And that greedy Antoine couldn't resist smoking them, even though my *m'mère* warned him not to. Any fool knows that our enemies can harm us if they get somet'ing in our mouths."

It took Jerralee a moment to realize the significance of Zareh's rambling speech. "You seem to know a lot about the old legend."

"Not legend, truth. My *m'mère* and later my *maman* tell me the story many times. I knew I would someday possess the magic to reverse the curse."

Jerralee wasn't sure she believed in voodoo, but she was superstitious enough to take a step away from Zareh. "That's very interesting."

"It is, *non?* My *m'mère* work' for Madame Delarue and was to marry with Belzac. He was the conjurer bought by your *p'père* Jules to make the curse. My *m'mère* tell Belzac she would not wed him if he work a curse on M'sieu Antoine. Belzac was all paid up when she try to stop the bad work. But he fix' it."

"He did? How?"

"He limit' the spell." Zareh explained the age limit for producing children. She did not, however, volunteer to tell Jerralee how the curse could be broken.

While Jerralee was digesting that bit of information, Zareh took her hand and led her over to the pool. "M'sieu Nic," she trilled smugly, "your guest, she has arrived."

Nic stood, shading his eyes with his hands. He wasn't expecting anyone. When he saw that the caller was Jerralee LeBeau he was frankly shocked. He thought he'd made it perfectly clear that he had no wish to talk to her: two could play at her little game.

For years she had pointedly avoided him, yet now that she wanted something here she was.

Good manners forced him to extend his hand as she approached, even as he wondered how Zareh could possibly have known the woman would come. "I must say this is a surprise, Mademoiselle LeBeau." Zareh caught his eye with a look that said it certainly was not.

Obviously uncomfortable, Jerralee shook his hand perfunctorily. She was dressed in snug blue jeans and a plain white blouse, but she needed no feminine adornment to emphasize her luscious figure. The balmy breeze, laden with the scent of magnolias and wisteria, fingered her blond shoulder-length hair. She reached up to smooth it, and the coy gesture irritated Nic. He knew Jerralee LeBeau was anything but coy.

"This is not a social call, Delarue." Jerralee wanted to make that clear.

"No, I did not think it was. Won't you sit down?" He led her to a white wrought-iron table in the shade of a gnarled old magnolia tree and offered her a chair.

"I will make somet'ing cool to drink." Zareh glided off toward the house.

As Nic pulled out Jerralee's chair, she caught the scent of coconut from the tanning oil slathered over his muscular shoulders. She told herself that the sudden flush of heat she felt was due to the humid late-summer weather and not to the unclad nearness of her host. He had draped a fluffy towel around his neck, but in her opinion, it was not adequate covering.

Nic sat across from her, and stretched his long legs alongside her chair. "Do you have it with you?"

Jerralee raised her eyes from his bronzed limbs and their gazes locked. "Do I have what with me?"

"The IOU. I assume that is the reason for your unexpected and inconvenient call." His dark gaze lowered and he appraised her openly, perversely enjoying her obvious discomfort. He had tried, countless times, in the past to get better acquainted with the illusive Mademoiselle LeBeau. But she had wanted nothing to do with him. He was glad that she'd come to him. Perhaps she realized the irony in the situation, as well. That would explain why she seemed as nervous and as ill at ease as a tart in church.

Jerralee felt her cheeks grow warmer. His scrutiny was insulting and exciting at the same time. His gaze returned to hers and the air was suddenly charged with incredible energy. Her stomach fluttered defensively at his lazy look. It definitely bordered on sexual aggression. Her anger flared again, and she blamed him. How was she supposed to concentrate on her mission when the man's swimsuit left so little to the imagination?

"Mr. Delarue—"

"Call me Nic," he commanded in the authoritative tone he usually reserved for business dealings.

Jerralee was disgusted with herself. She was not easily intimidated, but somehow Delarue had accomplished just that in the first few moments of their meeting. She adopted an equally formal tone. "Very well, *Nic*." Her emphasis indicated that she could think of other names to call him. "Would you put on some clothes?"

He smiled for the first time, amused by her legendary spunk. "Of course. If my body bothers you." But on the way to the house, he was seized by an unexpected and unwelcome desire to prolong Jerralee's visit.

Without quite knowing why, he turned back. "Zareh is preparing dinner. Won't you join me?"

"Thank you, no. I have plans tonight."

"How unfortunate." Accustomed to having his way, Nic was displeased at her refusal. But he was experienced in manipulating things to his advantage in business. And this was business, wasn't it?

"Due to the lateness of the hour, perhaps it would be better for us to meet at another time then," he remarked briskly.

Jerralee groaned inwardly. She didn't want to meet with him again. Ever. The traitorous way she felt when she was near him was too powerful and too maddening. She only wanted to get this meeting over with. She decided quickly that she could afford to pass up another one of Tante Olivette's arranged dates if it meant making progress on the IOU.

"No, I'll change my plans. May I use your telephone?"

"Of course. Zareh will take care of you while I shower and change."

Jerralee mentally tried to refine her IOU strategy as she followed him into the house, but found that she could not formulate any clear thoughts on that subject. In spite of herself, she felt her wayward gaze continually drawn to Nic Delarue's muscular backside. He possessed the sexiest behind she had ever seen.

Now where had that thought come from? she wondered, her frustration almost complete. The idea was obviously not her own. However, for a brief moment, she almost hated old Jules LeBeau for what he'd done to Nic Delarue. What a shameful waste of manhood!

Chapter Three

When Jerralee finished the unpleasant task of breaking yet another date, she looked up to find Zareh Dulac waiting silently at the study door.

"I know what an imposition an unexpected dinner guest can be. May I help you in the kitchen?"

"You were not unexpected, *chérie*. I knew you were coming and everyt'ing is ready." Zareh motioned Jerralee to a hunter-green wingback chair and took the one opposite for herself. "I will keep you company until M'sieu Nic comes downstairs."

"You've been with the Delarue family for as long as I can remember," Jerralee remarked.

"I've live' on this plantation all my life. I was M'sieu Nic's nanny, and when his *bébés* come, I will be their nanny, too."

"But what about the—"

"That will be reversed." Zareh's mindreading skills anticipated Jerralee's questions. "I have already set it in motion."

Jerralee knew without asking that the woman wouldn't divulge any secrets. Everything about her was mysterious. "Does Nic have any relatives?"

"Sadly, they are all gone. That curse was handed down from M'sieu Antoine to M'sieu Gaston to M'sieu Philippe and now to M'sieu Nic. But I will fix it, *non?*"

"I hope so," Jerralee replied, suddenly uncomfortable with her own ancestors' part in the whole wretched mess. "Didn't you say the curse was limited? It seems to me that the male Delarues would have been wiser to marry early and have as many children as possible before they reached thirty-five."

"Much wiser, yes. But M'sieu Nic married wrong and wasted his time. His first wife was afraid she would get fat, she was afraid of the pain. Skinny Justine was afraid of everyt'ing. She was even afraid of me. Is that not strange?" Her throaty laughter rumbled through the room.

Jerralee couldn't imagine why anyone *wouldn't* fear a woman who was on a first-name basis with all the local "two-headed" doctors, practitioners of voodoo. Curious, she blurted, "What did you do to her, Zareh?"

"Moi?" Her dark face spoke of unjust accusations. "I did not'ing. I only try to help her."

Jerralee grinned. "I'll bet you did."

"I made many potions, and a special one to keep her husband from straying, not that he ever did. M'sieu Nic is an honorable man. But a woman like that one need all the help she can get. I even gave her my secret mixture to keep her skin from wrinkle'. But did she use it? *Non.* She nag', nag', nag', poor M'sieu Nic allatime. That skinny wench want no *bébés,* no Long Shadows and finally she want no M'sieu Nic.''

"No marriage is better than a bad one," Jerralee pointed out. Which was exactly what she told her relatives when their interference became too much to bear.

"That's what M'sieu Nic say." Zareh grinned. "He say it again after Mam'selle Bettina, too."

Jerralee felt as guilty as if she'd been eavesdropping on a private conversation and hurriedly changed the subject. "The house is beautiful. Does Nic have many guests?"

"Not many, *non,*" Zareh replied thoughtfully as she tapped her pursed lips with a long blood-red fingernail. Treating Jerralee to another beaming smile, she added, "But now that you have come, he surely will."

"He will what?" Nic asked as he strode into the room, casually dressed in pleated white trousers and a soft blue shirt.

Jerralee hadn't thought it possible for a man to look sexier clothed than unclothed, but Nic Delarue did.

"Why do I get the distinct impression that you've been boring my guest by talking about me, Zareh?"

The woman laughed pleasantly and was halfway out of the room before giving her saucy answer. "Perhaps you have the power, too."

Nic and Jerralee engaged in stilted small talk until they were summoned to dinner a few minutes later. They passed through an opulent dining room furnished with a cherrywood table and twelve chairs dating from the turn of the century. The matching breakfront held a priceless collection of silver and crystal. Oil paintings of long-dead Delarues looked down from the silk-papered walls.

Nic's ancestors seemed to watch her reproachfully, and Jerralee silently apologized for her attire and for daring to enter such hallowed halls in the first place. Nic might not take the feud seriously, but his sour-faced ancestors certainly had.

Nic opened the French doors and led her outside to the garden, where a small table set with simple white china and waxy magnolia blossoms stood on the flagstone terrace.

"I hope you don't mind informality," he said. "I usually take my evening meals out here."

"It's beautiful." The sun was setting, and the evening had cooled. The sultry air was heavy with perfume from the flowers and alive with the trilling of hundreds of tree frogs. Beyond the rolling green lawn came the bellow of bullfrogs from somewhere in the swamp. Swagged with Spanish moss and older than memory, huge live oak trees cast the long shadows that had given the plantation its name. The mansion was a white-pillared monument to a way of life that was no more.

Nic's smile was enigmatic as he sat down across from her and Jerralee couldn't help thinking that perhaps Zareh was right about his power. He certainly possessed the ability to make her heart pound, no matter how hard she willed it to slow down. Even breathing was difficult and, to make matters worse, she was suddenly overcome by an irrational impulse to lean into those sensuous lips for a forbidden taste.

His smile vanished and he suddenly turned serious. "You have beautiful eyes," he said, as if it pained him to admit it. "They're as blue as the bayou, and as full of secrets."

Did men really say things like that to women? Jerralee wondered. None of the men she knew ever had, yet it sounded so grudgingly sincere coming from Nic. Before she could say or do anything, Zareh spoke behind her and Jerralee jumped in surprise. How *did* the woman sneak around so quietly?

Zareh set a dish of shrimp étouffée on the table and its spicy aroma mingled with the subtle fragrance of the garden.

"M'sieu Nic pay you a big compliment, Mam'selle." She filled their mint-garnished glasses with iced tea and added, "As a little boy, he love' to swim in that bayou. He was allatime begging to go skinny-dip' down there."

"I no longer beg for the things I desire, Zareh," he said, holding Jerralee's gaze with his own.

Zareh chided him. "But using the word 'please' sometime would not hurt you, I t'ink."

Nic chuckled merrily, and Jerralee unexpectedly envied the other woman's easy way with him. His laughter transformed him, giving her a momentary glimpse of the vulnerable man beneath the hard-edged facade. That revealing glimpse shook her more than anything had shaken her so far since she'd met Nic.

"I will go home now, M'sieu Nic," Zareh said. "I take care of the dishes in the morning, so don't get no ideas about messin' in my kitchen."

"I know the rules," Nic said indulgently.

"Not all of them. Not yet," she replied cryptically. "Good night Mam'selle LeBeau." Before Jerralee could reply, the woman disappeared.

Nic commented on her confusion as he passed Jerralee a dish of dirty rice. "Don't let Zareh get to you, she's really quite harmless."

"I think she's wonderful."

"You do?" he asked with surprise. "Few people take to her. She frightens them."

"She's very loyal to you. You're lucky to have such a staunch supporter."

"She is that. Sometimes I wish she wouldn't take such a personal interest in my private life, but I guess she's earned the right to meddle after so many years."

Recalling the purpose of her visit, Jerralee said, "About the IOU—"

"Please. Let's not discuss business over dinner. Zareh would not approve. Let's enjoy our meal and talk about the IOU later."

She didn't appreciate the delay, but deferred to her host. She certainly didn't want to earn Zareh Dulac's disapproval. When she crossed her legs under the little bistro-style table, her knees bumped his. "Sorry," she mumbled.

"My pleasure."

Throughout the meal, no matter what she did with her knees or legs, they somehow managed to come into direct contact with Nic's. So much "play" beneath the table distracted her from her food and could not be accidental. She wondered what it meant. Was he trying to keep her off guard? If that was his strategy, it was working.

"Doesn't Zareh live here with you?" she asked as she folded her napkin and gave up further pretense of eating. "You certainly have enough room."

"She lives on the grounds, but she has a house of her own farther down the bayou. She likes it that way, says it gives her the necessary privacy. To work her magic, you know."

Jerralee watched as Nic shifted in his chair. He had maneuvered his legs until her knees were sandwiched between them, and Jerralee sat extremely still, worried that if she moved one centimeter either way they might come into contact in a way far too intimate for enemies.

"Would you like something more, Jerralee? More tea? Or perhaps a little dessert? Zareh made a bread pudding with Chantilly cream."

"No thank you." The words were more vehement than necessary. She wasn't sure if she was turning down his offer of dessert or protesting the things that were happening beneath the pristine tablecloth.

Slowly and deliberately, while their gazes remained locked, Nic slid one of his long legs between hers and clasped her knee between his strongly-muscled thighs. He knew it was a bold move, but the need to touch her was irresistible.

Her leg imprisoned, Jerralee's heart beat frantically. Her whole body pulsed, matching the accelerated rhythm. Before she could banish the thought, she wondered how it would feel to be embraced by Nic. A sudden heat surged through her and offered new insight into the theory of spontaneous combustion.

With his gaze fixed on her mouth, Nic asked, "Have you had enough?"

"Yes," she breathed, and stood up quickly, in a hurry to get away from him. "I think I feel a headache coming on."

A headache, a heartache, an all-over bodyache. "I really should go," she said, almost pleadingly.

Nic stood. "Zareh makes a wonderful headache potion. Would you care to try it?"

Facing him, she barely managed to quell the superstitious impulse to cross her index fingers and hold them up before her, as if keeping a vampire at bay. There was a power at work here that she did not understand.

In a feeble attempt at humor, she asked, "A potion? Is it the wing-of-bat and eye-of-newt variety?"

"Nothing so exotic. Just a few herbs and roots, but it works wonders on nasty headaches."

"I think I'll pass. An early night will cure me."

"That's too bad. I was hoping to get a look at that IOU." Despite the unnerving feelings he was experiencing, Nic wasn't ready for the evening to end.

The IOU? Jerralee shook her head to clear it. What was wrong with her? How had she managed to forget the whole purpose of her visit? It was as though she'd stepped into a web of enchantment the moment she arrived at Long Shadows.

"Perhaps I am not so tired. A good strong *tasse* is what I need."

"Coffee? Of course. Zareh makes a wonderful *café brûlot*."

Together they gathered up the dishes and carried them into the kitchen. After pouring the coffee, Nic placed his hand at the back of her waist and escorted her into the study where she had waited for him earlier.

The high-ceilinged room held a small settee, two wingback chairs and an enormous teakwood desk. Prints of old steamboats in heavy frames lined the walls.

Jerralee assured herself that, although warm, Nic's touch was light and could hardly account for the quivering in her stomach or the vibrating awareness of her nerves. She blamed it on anxiety at finally getting down to business. Surely it was the coming confrontation making her so jumpy.

She watched as Nic added brandy to the mixture of coffee, spices and citrus peel. Then he lit the drink dramatically and allowed it to burn for a few moments before serving.

She sipped the hot brew, and tried to concentrate on a matter as mundane as money.

They relaxed in matching chairs, and the room grew ominously silent. She glanced up from the rim of her cup and found herself gazing into a pair of eyes that were a depthless shade of brown.

She had seen Nic around Poulee Crossing a thousand times, but never had she really *looked* at him. He was tall, but not too tall, and his body was fit and trim beneath the stylish cut of his silky, tailored shirt. His hair was a deep, rich shade of mahogany, and he'd brushed it back off his face. That face was a study in strength—high cheekbones, heavy eyebrows and strong, determined jaw.

His lips were full and sensual and bracketed by small creases. It was impossible to determine if those lines had formed from scowling or smiling. When he did smile—as he was doing now—it was with the self-assurance of a man who knew exactly what kind of an effect he had on a woman.

"You're staring, Nic," she said, deciding a good offense was the key to getting through the evening.

"Yes," he admitted readily. "I've never been so physically attracted to a woman before, and I'm trying to figure out why."

His honesty deflated her. "Is that a compliment?" If he was trying to charm her into forgetting about her mission, he would have to stop using recycled lines from romantic novels.

"I believe it's a paradox." Abruptly, Nic was in front of her chair, and Jerralee protested as he pulled her into his arms. But that protest turned into a soft sigh as she felt his lips lower onto hers. When she heard his answering moan, she melted against him. She was filled with a rare heat as his tongue gently traced the soft fullness of her lips. She was plunging into something far more complex than a business liaison, and she had no idea how far the wave of desire would carry her.

He caressed her breast through the soft fabric of her shirt and it surged at the intimacy. He deepened the kiss and she clung to him, even as her mind tried to regain some sense of reality. His hands in her hair, he drew her head back to expose the pulsing hollow at the base of her throat and he kissed her there, wonderingly. Then he tugged aside her collar to brush his lips along her shoulder, across her collarbone and onto the warm, satiny skin of the opposite shoulder.

Jerralee's body had betrayed her, and to stop now would be agony, but she pushed at his chest anyway.

"Stop it, Nic. You shouldn't have started this, and I should never have allowed it."

An expression of surprise flickered briefly across his handsome face, then disappeared. "Perhaps not, but that's how you affect me. God only knows why." His tone was self-mocking.

"Are you in the habit of acting on every primitive impulse you feel?" she demanded as she turned away from him.

Nic thought he was being strangely reasonable given the circumstances. He hadn't wanted to kiss her, had he? And when he had, her response had been more than he could have hoped for. On the other hand, his own response had been a real startler.

"Actually, I'm not. I usually possess unqualified restraint. At the risk of sounding like a cliché, I have to say that I don't know what came over me."

Jerralee could believe that. She didn't feel quite herself tonight, either.

"I believe in being honest," he said. "I think it's best to get these things out in the open so they can be dealt with."

"I happen to think it's better to ignore them and hope they'll go away." Jerralee scrambled to her feet. "Since we can't seem to stick to business, I think I'll leave. I need to feed Crevi."

"Ah yes, the infamous Crevi." The term was short for *écrevisse*. "Crawfish is a strange name for an alligator."

"He was very small when I found him."

"And now that he's not so small, can't he fend for himself?"

"Yes, but he still expects special treats from time to time."

"Anyone I know?"

She ignored the amused comment. "How did you know about Crevi?"

"People love to talk about your...ah...eccentricities."

How well she knew that. "Goodbye. I see now that coming here was a mistake."

"You don't like me much, do you?"

"I wouldn't say that," Jerralee said, hedging. In all honesty she *couldn't* say that.

"I am a Delarue. Is that a strike against me?"

"Maybe."

"Only maybe?"

At a loss, Jerralee reminded him, "I'm a LeBeau."

"At least we don't suffer from identity crises," he said wryly.

"We aren't supposed to like each other, and we are especially not supposed to be attracted to each other."

"Where is that written?"

"In family history."

Damned family history again. Nic had always been proud to be a Delarue, but being a poor nameless foundling suddenly seemed to have its advantages, too. "That is totally absurd. There is no reason why we shouldn't give in to our feelings."

On a primitive level Jerralee agreed with him, but pride wouldn't allow her to admit it. "Our families have been enemies for four generations."

Nic was fed up with all the nonsense of feuds, curses and magic. His patience suffered for it. "Fine, Mademoiselle LeBeau. We will continue at cross-purposes, if that will maintain your precious status quo. We'll feud so long and so hard that we'll go on record with the Hatfields and the McCoys. We'll make the Montagues and the Capulets look like rank amateurs. Is that what you want?''

Jerralee felt miserable. Comparing their situation to that of Romeo and Juliet did make the feud sound silly. But she'd held on to it for so long. It was the battle cry she used to rally her weakening willpower. She'd used it to fuel her resentment toward Nic Delarue and all he stood for. Without it, she'd have no defense against him.

"All I want is justice. You owe my family eighteen thousand dollars, and I mean to collect it by whatever means are available to me."

Nic's eyebrow quirked. "That sounds suspiciously like a threat."

"Make of it what you will." Her emotions had cooled. She wasn't angry anymore. Instead, she felt empty and sad. "I believe I'll follow your original suggestion and contact your attorney."

She grabbed her purse, and Nic followed her into a foyer that was dominated by a sweeping staircase and a crystal chandelier.

"About that IOU." If he couldn't tempt her body, he'd settle for tempting her greed. "I can't authenticate it if you won't show it to me."

Jerralee withdrew the fragile document from her handbag. "How will you validate the signature?"

"There are hundreds of old papers in the attic and some of them were signed by Theodule Delarue. But I'm afraid the attic contains two hundred years worth of accumulation and it may take time to locate the right documents."

"And you'll call me when you've found them?" she asked hopefully.

Nic shook his head. "I'm afraid not. I stand to gain nothing from this. My time is valuable. Do you really expect me to spend it searching the attic for your benefit?"

"Is that your subtle way of blackmailing me into helping you?"

"If I were trying to be subtle, you would not have seen through the ploy," Nic said dismissively. "Frankly, I don't want to spend hours digging around a dusty attic with, or without, the dubious pleasure of your company."

Jerralee had come here expecting resistance. But Nic's kiss had made her think he might be willing to help her. It hurt that he wasn't being cooperative, but she wouldn't let him know that. "So what do you want?"

He fingered the yellowed scrap of paper. "I want to know what you hope to gain by inventing this whole thing."

"Inventing? You think I faked the IOU?" It had never occurred to her that her motives might be suspect.

"The thought has crossed my mind. After all, an IOU that was previously unknown to anyone suddenly appears out of nowhere just when you need it most. Quite a coincidence."

"Coincidence is God's way of remaining anonymous," she quipped. "Besides, it's no more coincidental than the unexpected discovery of unknown stars and sunken treasures. Like the IOU, they were there all along, just waiting for someone to look in the right place."

There it was again. The fighting spirit that made Jerralee LeBeau so interesting. "I'll concede that point, madam," he said with a mock bow. He opened the door for her. "Too bad we couldn't work something out."

"My attorney thinks I have a very good case, and he's willing to take you to court if that's what we have to do."

"As you wish. But then I would have to call my legal representatives in Baton Rouge, and they'll probably advise me to do nothing to help you. It seems to me that the burden of proof is yours. Why should I cooperate?"

"If you don't, I sue."

"Fine. You'll have to consult expensive experts, and then my attorneys will call a whole battery of experts who could delay the settlement until doomsday."

Jerralee groaned inwardly. She couldn't afford a lengthy court battle, and he knew it. All his threats had been delivered in that charming, feudal lord voice of his, but they were threats all the same. She was tempted to tell him she'd see him in court, but changed her mind when she thought about the family. Most of them *did* depend on the Delarue Sugar Mill for employment. She couldn't allow her ego to endanger their livelihoods.

Besides, Hercule wouldn't stand a chance against those Baton Rouge pettifoggers. "You win this round," she said grudgingly.

Her choice of words signified that the fight wasn't over and that fact pleased Nic. Jerralee was not a woman to give up easily. "Are you willing to put forth a little effort to solve this dilemma?"

"Anything." At his amused look, she clarified, "*Almost* anything." She didn't particularly relish the thought of spending hours alone with him in a cramped attic, but if it would get him out of her life, she'd do it.

"I'm glad we could reach an understanding on this," he said sarcastically.

"Oh, we understand each other all right. But I don't mind telling you that I believe you have ulterior motives for wanting me back in this house, Delarue."

"Call me Nic," he countered, declining to deny her accusation. How could he when it was true?

"I think you are devious and underhanded."

He smiled at that, a sad, mysterious smile that tore at her heart. "What else could you expect from a Delarue?"

"Nic, I—"

"Good night, Jerralee," he interrupted. "I'll see you tomorrow night."

He opened the door and she escaped into the sultry, moonlit Louisiana night. She dashed down the front walk to the battered blue pickup truck parked in the wide circular driveway. MS. FIX-IT was emblazoned in uneven lettering on the side. The engine coughed and sputtered before roaring to life, and when it did, she aimed it down the avenue lined by giant live oak trees and disappeared in the enveloping darkness.

Nic sensed a presence in the room and whirled around to confront Zareh, who was standing quietly at the foot of the stairs. "I thought you went home."

"Somet'ing come up," she said evasively.

"An eavesdropping session perhaps?" he asked knowingly.

"Did you see the paper?"

"Yes."

"Is it real, do you t'ink?"

"I don't know yet."

"Will you pay?"

"I don't know that, either."

"Mam'selle Jerralee is a lovely woman, *non?*"

"Damnably so."

"When you are near her, do you feel the power?" Zareh's curiosity was obvious and all too gleeful.

His eyes narrowed. "And what power would that be, Zareh?"

"Oh, the power of new love, of course," she replied with a deceptively innocent look.

"You didn't put anything in that *étouffée*, did you?"

"*Moi*, M'sieu Nic? *Non.* You tol' me no potion, so no potion I make."

It suddenly occurred to Nic that Zareh's spells and entrancements might take other forms. His actions tonight had been unduly forward, and Jerralee's response to them most unexpected. Was it possible that some magical force was at play here?

No, that wasn't possible. Nic didn't believe in magic anymore.

Chapter Four

The next evening Jerralee arrived at Long Shadows promptly at seven o'clock. This time Nic didn't waste small talk trying to make her visit seem like a social call. After a perfunctory greeting he immediately led her up the stairs to the attic.

At the end of a third floor corridor he inserted an old-fashioned brass key into the lock of a heavy mahogany door. It swung open on creaky hinges, and he stepped inside to switch on a bare overhead bulb that apparently hadn't been changed since the Depression.

"The attic is at the top of these stairs." He led her up a dim, narrow passageway.

"You need a map to find your way around this place," Jerralee muttered grouchily as she followed him. Coming back here had been difficult, and she felt uncomfortable. She still wasn't sure what she was getting herself into.

Her inexplicably wanton behavior last night worried her as she'd never been worried before. She didn't want to spend a whole evening alone with Nic Delarue in the close quarters of an attic, but at least this time her guard was up. She would not allow herself to be drawn into anything that went against her better judgment.

Nic flipped on another light, illuminating the vast attic space at the top of the mansion. It was larger than Tante Olivette's whole house, and stacked to the rafters with boxes, trunks, old furniture and the debris of dozens of Delarue lives.

"This is it."

"You don't expect us to go through all of this tonight?" Jerralee surveyed the accumulated artifacts skeptically.

Nic suppressed a smug smile at her obvious dismay. If she thought getting what she wanted would be easy, she was in for a surprise. "It may take more than one night."

Jerralee groaned at the understatement and plopped down in a creaky wicker chair. "Are all those boxes filled with old papers?"

"Letters, journals, legal documents, even household receipts. The family never threw anything away."

"No doubt in the hope that someday a Delarue would distinguish himself enough to warrant saving it all for posterity," she said wryly.

"No doubt," Nic agreed as he handed her a dusty box to search. "Remember, we're looking for something signed by Theodule Delarue."

As if she needed reminding. The old IOU, tucked snugly into her purse, was the most important thing to happen to the LeBeau family in a hundred years. She wasn't likely to forget that. Opening a musty old expense ledger and turning to a yellowed page, she remarked on the low cost of corn so many years ago.

Nic looked up from his own search and smiled. "That's one of my grandfather's journals. In addition to recording household business, he also made personal entries."

Curious, Jerralee turned the yellowed pages. Without first scanning the content, she began to read aloud:

Yvette sickened today and took to her bed. I sent for the doctor, but it was too late, and the male child was born dead. There were complications, and this time I nearly lost her. The doctor says my wife can bear no more children, and she is convinced her loss is the result of the Delarue curse.

Jerralee stopped reading and glanced uneasily at Nic. The words had been written long ago, but the underlying pain had not faded with time, and she felt it acutely.

"Is that all?" he asked softly.

"No, there's more."

"Read it," he commanded.

Jerralee swallowed hard and read:

I can no longer scoff at the witch doctor's *maudire*. I exist because my mother was already *enciente* when my father was cursed. I was born two months later, but I have no brothers or sisters. By the grace of God, Yvette and I had a healthy son last year to carry on the Delarue line, at least for one more generation.

She glanced at Nic. "That baby was your father?"

"Yes."

"And you are the last Delarue."

"Perhaps not. I'm only thirty-four, so it's not too late yet," he teased.

She nodded, recalling the age limit on the curse.

Nic noticed her worried expression. "You don't believe in the curse do you, Jerralee?"

"I don't know what to believe," she answered truthfully. She shouldn't feel responsible for the size of his family, but somehow she did. "I don't want to, but all things being equal, you should have as many relatives as I have."

"Now that *would* be a curse," he said. A dark eyebrow that was lifted in amusement lessened the sardonic effect of his words.

Taking umbrage at the implied slur on her own family, due to its size, Jerralee glared at him and returned her attention to the papers. Why should she feel sorry for Nic Delarue? Except for family, he had everything he could possibly want. The LeBeaus had precious little, and yet he was determined to possess that as well. It would pay to remember that whenever her traitorous feelings softened toward him.

Just when she had worked up a fair amount of renewed resentment, he spoke again. "I don't want to father children just to continue the family name. That would be self-serving, wouldn't it? When I have children, it will be because their mother and I wish to create a living extension of our love."

Jerralee noted that he used the word "when," not "if," in referring to future fatherhood. Such optimism had to be admired. Determined to complete her task and get away from Nic before admiration could turn into something more potent, she continued the search with renewed vigor.

They worked in silence for a while, opening dusty boxes and sifting through the contents, looking for anything that might have Theodule Delarue's signature on it.

"Theodule *could* write his name, couldn't he?" she asked peevishly an hour later. No one had ever accused her of having a long attention span, and her exasperation was growing with each passing minute.

"As far as I knew, he was literate," Nic answered without looking up from the stack of papers on his lap. He was dressed casually in a pair of faded jeans and a white cotton shirt. The long sleeves were rolled back on tanned forearms lightly sprinkled with dark hair. He was seated cross-legged on the oak floor, and a beguiling lock of hair had fallen down over his forehead.

Jerralee didn't want to be fascinated by Nic Delarue, but something about him drew her gaze. She watched him surreptitiously while pretending to sift through papers.

The last rays of sunset shone through small leaded glass windows set high under the eaves of the attic and pooled around Nic like a well-placed stage light. When he stirred, millions of dust motes danced attendance around him and the air seemed charged with the quiet energy of the man commanding the space. Long moments ticked by and Jerralee felt herself entranced, but she blamed it on the hypnotic effect of his aristocratic hands flipping rhythmically through a stack of pages.

She noticed a smear of dust on his left cheek and the little smudge captured her attention. Unaware of where the urge came from, she longed to reach out and tenderly wipe it away. To gently smooth back his tousled hair. To feel the crisp texture of his shirt against her skin. To know the warmth of his embrace. The sudden need to touch Nic in some way was so powerful that Jerralee had to fight the urge by gripping the sides of her chair with both hands.

She gave herself a mental shake. What was the matter with her? Such fanciful thoughts were totally unlike her. She was a doer, not a dreamer. A realist, not a romantic. After careful thought she decided that her imagination had taken flight due to the tedious nature of her present task.

There was too much at stake for her to lose interest in the project so soon. But it was discouraging that they had barely scratched the surface and had so many more hours of searching ahead of them.

She put aside the box she'd been looking through and got up to stretch her cramped muscles. She wandered around, poking curiously—and unabashedly—into Delarue privacy. In one trunk she found a treasure trove of vintage clothing, some dating back to the twenties.

Pulling out a feathered cloche hat and a wicked black-beaded shimmy dress, she mentally compared the expensive clothes with the hand-me-down floursack dresses the LeBeau women had undoubtedly worn during the same period. They'd left no legacy for future generations. Their dresses had been worn and washed and patched until they fell apart, because the owners had possessed no others.

This sixty-five-year-old gown looked almost new because the spoiled, rich Delarue woman who had bought it had deigned to wear it only once. A lifetime of penny-pinching made it impossible for Jerralee to understand the kind of economic freedom that allowed such self-indulgent excess.

"Do you like that dress?" Nic's voice startled her.

"It's a little gaudy for my tastes," she lied. In truth, she found it beautiful for the romantic Gatsby-ish images it evoked.

"It appears to be about your size," he remarked. "Why don't you keep it?"

"I have plenty of clothes, thank you." She glanced uneasily down at the worn denim overalls that contradicted her. She'd worn her work clothes because she hadn't wanted Nic to think she had primped for his benefit. Now she wished she'd taken more care with her appearance.

"I didn't mean to imply otherwise. I only thought to give you the dress." Nic couldn't understand Jerralee's defensiveness. Couldn't the woman accept a simple gift? Or perhaps it was the fact that the offer came from him that she found so distasteful.

"I don't need any handouts from you."

"Of course, you don't."

"Besides, where would I wear such a silly dress? Crawfishing on the bayou?" She quickly folded the gown back into its protective tissue paper wrapping. Nic's offer did not warrant her sarcasm, but it served to remind her of the vast differences between his background and hers.

"I never meant to offend you, Jerralee."

His quiet tone, when she least expected understanding, made her regret her lack of graciousness. "Let's get back to work, okay?" She shut the trunk with a thud and began looking through another box.

"As you wish."

A few minutes later she found something that surprised her. "There's a Santa suit in this one." The costume was old, but lovingly preserved.

"Don't look so shocked. Delarues believe in Christmas, you know. That suit's been in the family for years."

She examined it closely. "It isn't even dusty. It's been worn recently," she said in an accusing tone.

"Yes, Detective LeBeau. If you must know, I wore it to the mill's last Christmas party."

"You play Santa at the party?"

Nic mock-frowned at her consternation. "Exactly how low is your opinion of me anyway? I suspected that you found me a wastrel and a scoundrel, but I had no idea your loathing went so far."

His apparent amusement at her expense made the heat rise in Jerralee's face, but an apology wouldn't come. "I just never dreamed you would play Santa for a bunch of millhands' children."

He was unaccustomed to justifying his actions to anyone, but for some reason he wanted her to understand. "I like the kids and I love their excitement. Using that disguise is also the only way I can attend the party and watch my employees have a good time. If they knew I was there, it would put a damper on their fun."

She nodded. *That* she could understand. Everyone would be so busy deferring to "M'sieu Nic" that they would lose the party spirit.

"I went to the annual picnic once," he continued. "But for some reason, my presence made everyone uncomfortable. I made up an excuse about a previous engagement and left early. I never attended after that. Then, a few years ago, the hired Santa got sick before the Christmas party and I couldn't find a substitute. I didn't want to disappoint the children, so I dug this suit out and went in his place. No one knew I was Santa, and they all had a good time."

Jolly beneficence didn't fit the image Jerralee had of Nic Delarue, and the unexpected contradiction made her uncomfortable. "Are you sure you don't use it as an excuse to spy on your employees?"

Her question struck him like an unexpected dart, but Nic maintained his composure. "I can assure you, I have no ulterior motives when it comes to Christmas."

This time an apology *did* seem in order. "I'm sorry—"

"Forget it. I'd appreciate it if you would keep my little secret. If not for my sake, then for the sake of the children."

She felt properly chastised and nodded her agreement. She had mixed feelings about learning that Nic Delarue was a nice man. A kind man who cared about his employees. A rich man who gave joy to less privileged children and asked for no recognition or thanks. She had never expected him to have integrity, but she was strangely glad that he did.

She glanced at him and his gaze caught and boldly held hers. The slow heat that rose between them made it hard to remember their differences. Their past hostilities. Their present problems. As if bewitched, Jerralee forgot about the long feud between the Delarues and the LeBeaus and was conscious only of an overwhelming desire to kiss the man who had so entranced her.

Sensing Jerralee's turbulent feelings, Nic took a step toward her. He was compelled to act on the stunning impulses he felt. It didn't matter that this brash woman had been a thorn in his side for years.

Zareh's amused voice in the doorway stopped him cold. "I hope I am not interrupting anyt'ing. I t'ought you two might have worked up an appetite by now, *non?*" Setting a laden silver tray on a table, she gave Nic a saucy wink that told him just what kind of appetites she hoped had been stimulated.

"Thank you, Zareh." The timely interruption offered Nic a chance to regain control.

"I am going home now, M'sieu Nic, so you two will be all alone," Zareh trilled. "Good night, Mam'selle Jerralee." With another knowing look, she disappeared down the narrow stairway. The heavy door at the bottom of the steps swung shut firmly behind her.

Zareh's unexpected appearance defused the supercharged moment, and Jerralee and Nic pretended that nothing had almost happened. They sipped lemonade and munched pecan cookies as they quietly resumed their search, both careful to keep their minds, and their hands, occupied.

Some time later Nic yawned and pushed aside the papers he was perusing. "I'm going down to the kitchen for coffee. Would you care for a cup?"

Jerralee stood and stretched. "That sounds great. I'll come with you. If I don't move around some, I'll go to sleep."

Falling into step behind him she trod down the short stairway. At the landing Nic turned the brass knob, but the heavy door did not swing open. He frowned and twisted it again.

"What's wrong?" she asked.

"I don't know. The door seems to be stuck."

"Maybe it's locked. Don't you have the key?"

He nodded and fished into his pocket. "I thought I had it." He patted front and back pockets, but didn't find the elusive brass key.

"Did you leave it in the keyhole?" Jerralee asked.

"I must have. But it's so dim in here I can't be sure."

She flattened herself against the wall as he squeezed past her and sprinted up the stairs. In a moment he was back with a sheet of paper and a thin metal pick.

"What's that?"

"A buttonhook. And a key rescuer." He slid the piece of paper under the door and poked the buttonhook into the keyhole. Nothing happened. Nic looked confused.

"No key?" she asked.

"No key."

"So where is it?"

"How should I know?"

"You had it," she pointed out.

"Maybe I dropped it somewhere upstairs. Let's go up and look for it."

Fifteen minutes of frantic searching turned up nothing but dust.

"Well, that's just great," Jerralee grumbled. "All I need is to get locked in an attic with you."

"Won't you please try to control your excitement?" Nic was equally dismayed at the prospect.

She glared at him, jogged back down the stairs and started pounding on the locked door. "Maybe Zareh is still in the house. Help me yell."

He groaned as he joined her. Zareh. Of course. That explained a few things. He was positive he had left the door unlocked when he'd entered. He was also positive that he had left the key in the keyhole. Only one person could have locked the door and taken the key. Zareh. Her actions were clear, but her motives were still a bit muddy.

"Save your breath," he told her. "We can't count on Zareh to bail us out of this one."

"So what are we going to do?"

Nic folded his arms across his chest and said in his best CEO voice, "I will now entertain motions from the floor."

She eyed the heavy door. "Break it down."

Nic laughed, but there was more consternation than humor in it. "Oh, right."

"If you don't think you can do it alone, I'll help you." She pushed up the sleeves of her turtleneck shirt.

Nic grasped the back of her overalls and pulled her away. "Oh, no you don't. That happens to be a custom-made mahogany door, imported from Jamaica in the 1850s. It was built to withstand hurricane winds. We are *definitely* not going to break it down."

"We can try."

"All you'll succeed in doing is hurting yourself. Forget it."

She threw up her hands in disgust and stomped up the stairs. "Well, this is just great!"

He was right behind her. "Don't think I like it any more than you do."

Her eyes narrowed suspiciously. "I wouldn't be a bit surprised if you were hiding the darn key."

Her words were so unexpected that Nic's eyes widened in response. "Why in heavenly hell would I do that?"

"To keep me here against my will," she said brazenly.

He put his fists on his hips and laughed. "Lady, you have been sorely misled if you think I have to lock women in the attic to hold their interest."

He glared at her and was so handsome, so overwhelmingly masculine, that Jerralee knew he had a right to laugh. But she wasn't about to back down now. "Maybe not *other* women."

"Not you, either." Desire pulsed through Nic and he had a crazy, misguided urge to kiss her until her pouting lips trembled. This time there was no one, and nothing, to stop him.

He caressed her cheek with one hand and drew his thumb back and forth over the lips that taunted him. Her blue eyes widened and her pupils dilated. That age-old sign of interest was all the encouragement he needed. His other hand grasped her waist and pulled her against him.

Jerralee made no move to stop him. Her curiosity was too profound. Willfully, beseechingly, his mouth lowered to hers. His tongue teased her lips until they parted, then dipped warmly inside.

What followed was the sweetest, most devastating kiss Jerralee had ever had. It was a roller-coaster ride of a kiss. An earthquake of a kiss. A kiss fated to alter reality and change the course of human events.

It was magic.

Like all the clichés in all the silly love songs she'd ever heard, Jerralee felt her body responding to Nic's in unfamiliar ways. Her raw nerves pricked her, her fevered skin warmed her and her trembling heart and tortured breathing threatened to come to a dead stop.

This cannot be happening to me, she thought. But only for a moment, because all her energy was channeled into feeling and such singularity of purpose precluded thinking.

Nic tightened his hold on her and deepened the kiss. He felt her hands in his hair as she responded to him and he was gratified and excited. When his pleasure became painful he reluctantly drew away from her. An endearing, wondering sigh escaped her lips as they parted.

He looked down at her flushed face and smiled. Something amazing had just happened. He wasn't quite sure what it was, but it had aroused his most tender feelings, and that was no easy task.

Jerralee slowly opened her eyes and stared up at Nic, still mystified. Finally, her physiology returned to normal and she was surprised to discover that she had not lost the ability to speak. "Don't ever do that again."

He smiled at her stubborn reassertion of will. "Sorry, but I can't promise that."

"Why not?" she demanded. It was weak, but still a demand.

"Because I never make promises that I know I'll have to break," he said in a lazy, sexy voice.

Rendered momentarily speechless by the suggestiveness of his words, Jerralee spun around and began a wild search of the attic.

"What are you doing?" he asked with mild interest.

"I'm getting out of here. I refuse to spend even one more hour in your insufferable company."

"And how do you propose to leave?"

"I'm going to find something with which to break down that door."

"No. That you will definitely not do."

"All right." She turned to face him, her hands on her hips. "Since your heirloom door is so precious to you, I'll break out a window, instead. Unless, of course, they are all made of sacred glass, hand-blown by sixteenth century Tibetan monks."

"Nothing so exotic as that, I'm afraid. But just how do you plan to get out the window once you've broken it?"

She glanced up at the row of octagonal windows in question and sighed in frustration. They were even smaller than she remembered. An anorexic dachshund might be able to squeeze through one of them, but an adult human certainly could not.

"Any more bright ideas in that fertile imagination of yours?" he asked with mock cheerfulness.

She recognized defeat when it smacked her in the face. "No."

"Since we're going to be here all night, I suggest we make the best of a bad situation and get back to work." He turned away from her and hefted another box out of the endless stack of boxes.

"All night?" Jerralee stared at Nic's back as he bent down on one knee to look through the contents of the carton. Though slender, his body was unmistakably fit. His lightweight shirt revealed taut muscles in his shoulders and back. His softly faded jeans sheathed long thighs and molded trim buttocks. For the first time she noticed that he was not wearing socks with his loafers and she was surprised. For some reason, she never would have expected such informality from a Delarue.

"It appears so." His words interrupted her unabashed inventory. "I hope you're not afflicted with a weak constitution."

She grimaced at the reminder that there were no bathroom facilities available. "I can't stay here all night. What will people think?"

"What people do you mean?"

He didn't bother to turn around, and his apparent indifference to their situation only made her more indignant. "My Tante Olivette, for one."

Nic carefully concealed his smile from Jerralee. "Surely, you have spent the night with a man before?"

"I most certainly have not!" she declared indignantly.

He clucked his tongue sympathetically. "And I thought you were a liberated woman. Obviously, I was mistaken."

"A woman can be liberated without being loose."

"I agree. But a truly liberated woman doesn't worry about the opinion of others, so long as she is true to herself."

"Are you implying that I am a hypocrite?"

His wide shoulders raised in a shrug, but still he did not look at her. "All I'm saying is that you seem to want people to think you're unconventional when in reality you are a terribly traditional woman."

"I am not," she protested.

"Yes, you are. You have a pet alligator and operate a traditionally male business, which I agree is somewhat unusual in this parish. But Crevi and the fix-it shop are a facade you hide the real Jerralee behind."

"You don't know anything about me." She didn't like the direction this conversation was taking.

"Not nearly enough," he agreed amiably.

"What makes you such an expert on women anyway?" she wanted to know.

"Experience," he said. "And observation."

"Then maybe you've observed that in Poulee Crossing gossip can ruin a reputation."

"Gossip is the refuge of small minds," he told her philosophically. He was enjoying the exchange and becoming more intrigued by the moment. Having a conversation with Jerralee was like eating a good gumbo—the spice defined the flavor.

"You really are insufferable," she said in exasperation.

He smiled again. But again he was careful not to reveal his amusement to his irresistible fellow prisoner. "So you said."

Chapter Five

Jerralee gave up the search for evidence of Theodule Delarue's signature around midnight. She told herself that she didn't really care about Nic's unsolicited opinions, but his accusations bothered her.

She didn't like being called a hypocrite when she had always prided herself on her honesty and integrity. She spoke her mind and no one ever had to wonder where she stood on any issue. She'd never thought of Crevi and the fix-it shop in the way Nic had suggested—as superficial signs of unconventionality that she used to hide the fact that she was really as old-fashioned as any woman on the bayou. At least, she hadn't thought of it that way until Nic had brought it up.

Maybe she wasn't as liberated as she thought. She'd always considered herself a rebel at heart, but when it came to actually doing something contrary to her upbringing, she clung to tradition. And tradition said that an unmarried woman, no matter what her age, did not spend the night with a man, no matter what the circumstances.

There was nothing wrong with tradition, and she blamed her sudden soul-searching on Nic. Before meeting him, she'd had no reason to question herself or her motives. She had been accepting of life, happy and blissfully free from introspection. These nagging doubts were all his fault.

She found a patchwork quilt in a trunk and made herself comfortable in a corner, as far away from Nic's observant eyes as possible.

"Settling in for the night?" he asked inquisitively.

"Do I have a choice?"

"No." He put aside the carton he'd been searching and strode across the bare floor. He retrieved another quilt from the trunk and spread it out near Jerralee's makeshift bed. The colorful quilts made the boundaries of their respective territories quite clear and, given their verbal sparring, it seemed appropriate for them to square off in such a manner.

"Are you comfortable?" he asked solicitously.

"Not very," she grumbled.

"I hope you aren't worried about succumbing to your passions during the long night ahead," he teased.

She shot him a disgusted look. "I'll try to control myself."

"Well, your forehead is all wrinkled. You must be worried about something."

"I was just thinking how to explain this situation to my family."

"Why don't you tell the many LeBeaus that you were held prisoner against your will," he suggested with a playful smile.

"Which is not too far from the truth," she pointed out.

He frowned thoughtfully. "However, if you do that, one of your more honorable cousins may feel obliged to challenge me to a duel."

"I don't need my cousins to defend my honor," she retorted. "I can take care of myself."

"No doubt." He grinned again. "Maybe you can claim a memory loss. Or stand on the Fifth Amendment."

"Or I could plead temporary insanity," she quipped. "I must have been crazy to come here tonight."

"There is another possibility that probably hasn't occurred to you."

"And that is?"

"You could tell the truth."

She appeared to consider his suggestion. "No," she answered at last. "I'd rather confess to being beamed up by extraterrestrials than admit I spent the night with you."

Nic's unexpected boom of laughter startled him as much as it did her.

"I'm glad someone is having fun around here," she said huffily.

"Oh, I am." His unrestrained laughter finally bottomed out to a few mild guffaws. He'd laughed more tonight than he had in a month and it felt good, both physically and psychologically. He recalled reading somewhere that one of the best measures of mental health was the ability to laugh at oneself in a gently mocking way. Being with Jerralee changed his perspective and enabled him to see himself in an entirely different way.

He couldn't remember the last time he'd enjoyed a woman's company as much as he enjoyed hers. She was so refreshingly honest that he couldn't help being invigorated by her infectious spirit. She wasn't coy or flirtatious, seductive or manipulative. He wasn't quite sure what she was yet, but she was uniquely Jerralee.

It was a clear indication of her amazing personality that, in the short time he'd known her, she had somehow managed to shake him out of long-term complacency. A complacency he was only now becoming aware of. By helping him laugh at himself, she had unwittingly demonstrated that he was guilty of letting work and self-imposed isolation crowd the pleasure from his life.

Maybe Zareh really did know more about what was right for him than he did himself. Instead of scolding her for "accidentally" locking him in the attic with Jerralee, perhaps he would thank her, instead.

"I think you'd have fun, too," he said. "If you'd forget for a moment that you're a LeBeau and I'm a Delarue." His tone was serious now, his glance speculative.

She leaned across the quilt and rested her chin in her upturned palm. "Are you saying we should forgive and forget?"

"That would be a start."

"And where would we go from there?" she wanted to know.

"I have a number of interesting ideas on that subject." He inched toward her, drawn by the alluring scent of her floral perfume and by the unspoken invitation in her eyes.

"Are you planning to share any of those ideas with me?" She tried for sarcasm, but the breathlessness of her words spoiled the effect.

"All of them, if we have time." His lips captured hers in another tender kiss. How could a woman be so sweet? he wondered. How could she act so tough and yet feel so soft?

Jerralee melted against him for a brief moment before mustering the energy to pull away. "Get off my quilt," she whispered.

He pretended to carefully examine the coverlet in question. "This quilt is in my house. It was made by my grandmother. Yes, this is definitely a Delarue quilt."

"Possession is nine-tenths of the law," she pointed out.

"Thanks for reminding me." He wound his fingers in her hair, eased her back into his arms and claimed her mouth again.

The lingering kiss was warm and full of promise. As much as Jerralee hated to admit it, Nic Delarue was an exceptionally fine kisser. Instinctively varying the intensity of the embrace, he was rough and gentle by turn as his hands and lips sought—and gave—pleasure.

"What was that?" she whispered against his lips.

"I'm not sure it has a name," he sighed. "It's just something I've perfected over the years."

"Not the kiss, dummy. That noise."

"I didn't hear anything." He was too busy ravishing to notice much else.

"It sounded like a car engine."

"Impossible. Who would come all the way out here at this time of night?" Nic was less interested in midnight callers than he was in the business at hand, which at the moment happened to be the business of smothering Jerralee's neck with fervent little kisses.

For a few moments the only sounds were of the heavy breathing variety. Then the unmistakable boom of a backfiring engine shattered the silence.

"There it goes again. Didn't you hear it?" she demanded.

Nic released her so abruptly that she fell back on the quilt. "I heard it all right. It was definitely a car."

She scrambled to her feet and began stacking boxes and trunks into a precarious stairway.

He eyed the shaky structure dubiously. "Where did you study engineering? Wile E. Coyote University?"

"Shut up and help me," she commanded.

He rolled his eyes doubtfully, but decided to comply so that she wouldn't kill herself. As soon as they got the arrangement to her liking, she climbed up to look out the high windows.

Following her up the shaky pile, Nic perched cautiously on the stack of boxes beside her and peered out into the moonlit night. "You were right. There *is* someone out there."

He started to tap on the glass to attract the unlikely visitor's attention.

"Stop!" she yelled.

"Stop? When help is but a yell away? Now's your big chance to effect a macho rescue. Take off your shoe and break the glass."

"No. Be quiet."

Now he was perplexed. "Why?"

"That's Pete Nooley's truck."

"So?"

"I don't want him to know I'm here. His wife, Althea, is the worst gossip in town."

"At the risk of repeating myself, so?"

"Everything Althea Nooley knows, the whole parish knows in a matter of hours."

"That's ridiculous." He raised his hand to pound on the glass, but she grabbed his arm.

"I mean it, Nic."

"Don't be silly. This may be our only chance to get out of here tonight. Besides, Pete must have a good reason for coming around so late."

Jerralee was adamant. "He's probably looking for Zareh."

"At this time of night?"

"He works the second shift at the flyswatter factory," she explained.

"Why would he be looking for Zareh?"

"She makes a potion for his lumbago."

"How do you know that?" he asked.

She glared at him. "I told you, his wife is a gossip."

Nic sighed. "I thought you found the idea of spending the night with me repugnant."

"I do."

"But you'd rather do that than let anyone know you were consorting with the enemy. Is that it?"

She couldn't meet his eyes. His accusation was too close to the truth.

"Doesn't your family know you were coming here?"

"I didn't tell them. I didn't want to get their hopes up anymore about the IOU until we found a copy of Theodule's signature."

"Where do they think you are tonight?"

"We liberated women don't have to file an itinerary before leaving home," she said sarcastically.

"Pete will see your truck and tell his wife," he pointed out. "If what you say is true, your aunt and uncle will have the news before cockcrow."

"He won't see a thing. I parked around back behind the wisteria arbor."

Nic frowned. "Heaven forbid a passerby might see it and deduce that you were visiting me," he said scornfully. He'd been wrong to assume they had reached any kind of an understanding. Obviously, she still took the feud very seriously, which only proved how rigid and uncompromising she really was.

Jerralee looked out the window and saw Pete Nooley walk up to the front door. He must have knocked, but from where she was she couldn't be sure. When there was no answer he returned to his truck. The asthmatic old engine backfired again as he drove away.

"That was dumb," Nic told her when the truck was out of sight. "Stubborn, wrongheaded and just plain dumb. When you don't come home tonight, your aunt and uncle will assume you've been kidnapped or worse."

"No, they won't."

"They'll call the sheriff, who will have to get out of bed to investigate your mysterious disappearance. I can assure you he will not be happy about that."

"I suppose you know the sheriff personally?"

"As a matter of fact, I do."

"They won't call the sheriff," she told him as she climbed down from the window.

He followed, continuing the harangue. "I cannot believe how selfish and insensitive you are. It's bad enough to worry your relatives unnecessarily, but to waste the sheriff's time and the taxpayers' money on a wild-goose chase is unforgivable."

"Tante Olivette and Nonc Albert will not call the sheriff!" she shouted. She retreated to her quilt, resigned to spending what was left of the night in his company.

"What makes you so sure of that? Are you in the habit of disappearing without a word?"

To control her anger she closed her eyes and slowly counted to five in French. When she thought she had it under control, she answered, "Yes. As a matter of fact, I am. Not that I owe you an explanation, but I often go out to my father's old fishing shack in the swamp when I want to be alone."

"Why?"

"When you have a family as large and well-meaning as I have, sometimes the only way to escape their interference is to simply disappear."

"You go out in the swamp alone?" he demanded. "At night?"

"Yes."

"That's—"

"Dumb?" she finished for him. She plopped down on her quilt.

"And dangerous. Just where is this secret hideout of yours?" Nic didn't like to contemplate all the things that could go wrong for a woman alone in the swamp.

"If I told you, it wouldn't be a secret anymore, would it?" she asked with some of her old sass. "Besides, it's none of your business."

Nic didn't know why he bothered to care. Jerralee LeBeau was the most exasperating woman he'd ever met. He couldn't understand her, and that was the most exasperating thing of all.

"You're right," he agreed. "What you do is no concern of mine."

"I'm glad we agree on one thing."

"It may well be the only thing we will ever agree on."

She glanced at him uneasily and wondered if that was a threat about the IOU. She could read nothing in his closed expression. "You really are—"

"Insufferable?" he supplied with false cheer.

"Exactly." Jerralee tried to match Nic's phony amiability because she didn't want him to know just how upset she was. She never should have come here and she never should have asked a Delarue for help. It was obvious that they had too many personal conflicts to ever deal with each other on a business level.

She desperately wanted to question him further about the IOU and his ulterior motives regarding the purchase of Sweetwood. She was even willing to grovel a bit if it would help the family's cause. But before she could say anything more, Nic stretched out on his quilt, rolled onto his side and presented his back to her.

"Good night," he said with a ringing finality that left no room for further discussion.

No longer willing to grovel—even for her beloved family—Jerralee laid down, rolled onto her side and presented *her* back to him. "Good night."

Despite a fitful sleep Jerralee awakened early the next morning. She sat up and glanced at her watch; it was almost six o'clock. She wondered what time Zareh reported for work and how long it would take her to discover the unwilling prisoners.

Sometime during the night Nic had rolled close to her and was sleeping soundly on her quilt, his hands tucked beneath his chin like a little boy. A delicate ray of pale sunshine gleamed through the high windows and bathed him in a buttery glow much like that of a saint in an old painting. In fact, with his beautifully chiseled features and softly curved lips, he did look saintly.

Jerralee knew he was anything but.

They had gone to sleep angry last night, but this morning she had a hard time recalling what she'd been so mad about. She wondered if Nic had that effect on everyone or if she was the only one who responded to him that way.

As she watched him she remembered how warm his big body had felt when he'd held her, how exciting his kisses had been. Again she wondered what gave him so much power over her. Would she ever figure it out, or was it destined to remain one of life's little mysteries?

He stirred, stretched and opened his eyes. His "good-morning" was far more gracious than his "good-night" had been. Jerralee hoped he had also forgotten his anger.

"Did you sleep well?" she asked.

"That's my line," he said with a grin. "I'm the host."

She smiled at the euphemistic term. "If you must know, the floor was hard. *Exceptionally* hard."

"Any other complaints?"

"It's stuffy in here, the room service is deplorable and the plumbing is nonexistent."

"You look pretty in the morning," he said with unexpected sincerity.

"I do?"

"Very." Nic's eyes were greedy as he took in her soft, rumpled hair, her wide blue eyes. "Hasn't a man ever told you that before?"

"No."

Nic was pleased by her answer. As maddening as she could be, he wanted to be the only man to wake up with her. Perhaps he'd only kissed her last night, but in his dreams he'd done much more. He stood up before he could act on the unseemly urge to turn the dream into reality.

"Let's go downstairs and listen for Zareh," he suggested.

When she extended her hand he pulled her to her feet and almost into his arms. She stepped away from him quickly, though, and pretended to look for her purse. When she found it she followed him down the narrow steps to the attic door.

"I don't hear anything," she said after a few seconds of listening.

"So why are you whispering?" He bumped against the brass knob and was surprised when it moved. It turned easily in his hand. He looked up and Jerralee's questioning eyes met his.

"It's not locked?" she asked.

"Apparently not." He pushed open the door and they stepped out onto the upstairs landing. "I don't believe this."

Her eyes narrowed with suspicion. "Neither do I."

"Last night when we tried this door it was definitely locked." He couldn't understand what had happened.

"So you said." She brushed past him and headed for the front door. "Really, Delarue. I'm surprised you'd stoop to something so juvenile."

"What are you talking about?"

"'Oh, the door's locked' must be a variation of the 'Oh, we must be out of gas' trick. I haven't heard that one since high school."

He raced down the stairs beside her. "You don't think I faked the whole thing?"

She stopped abruptly and turned to face him. "A lot of the antebellum plantations are said to be haunted. Is Long Shadows favored with a resident ghost by any chance?"

"Not that I know of."

"Well, that rules out supernatural intervention," she said with feigned brightness. "Since there is no other likely explanation, I guess I 'think' you faked the whole thing." She tried to remember if she had attempted to open the door herself last night, or if she had merely taken his word that it was locked.

"You don't really believe that," he said incredulously.

She hurried down the stairs, angry at herself for being such a fool. "Good day, Mr. Delarue."

"Call me Nic," he taunted. "After all, we did spend the night together."

"Don't remind me." She dashed into the foyer where she nearly collided with Zareh Dulac. The housekeeper didn't seem at all surprised to see a woman running downstairs at such an unseemly hour. Apparently Nic often entertained female guests overnight and sent them packing the next day.

"Leaving so early, Mam'selle LeBeau?" Zareh asked pleasantly.

"Not nearly early enough," she replied as she sailed by the housekeeper.

"I have just put on the breakfast," Zareh called after her. "Won't you stay for a bite?"

Jerralee stopped at the door and turned around to face Nic. She tried to read his expression, but again she failed. Had he really tricked her into spending the night with him? But why? As he had pointed out, he did not need to keep women in his home against their will.

And if he wasn't responsible, who—or what—was?

She didn't understand what was going on, but she knew she had to get away from Long Shadows and its owner as fast as she could.

"No thank you, Zareh. But bon appétit," she said as she opened the door and stepped out into the lush Louisiana sunshine.

Chapter Six

Jerralee returned home to lots of hugs and a few raised eyebrows. She had considered all possible explanations for her overnight absence, but in the end she had chosen to tell the truth. Not because of Nic's influence, she assured herself, but because it would only be a matter of time before she cracked under her aunt's relentless questions.

Tante Olivette's own eyebrows raised to all-new heights when she learned that Jerralee had spent the night with Nic Delarue in his attic.

While telling her story, Jerralee inadvertently mentioned Pete Nooley's midnight visit. Too late, she realized she had carried the honesty thing too far and hastily dubbed the whole incident an "unfortunate accident."

Tante Olivette had her own thoughts on the subject. "If it is true that you dislike Nic Delarue so much, why did you not call out for help when Pete Nooley came around?''

Jerralee rolled her eyes heavenward. "And have the whole parish speculating about what a LeBeau was doing in a Delarue's attic in the first place?"

"I see." Tante Olivette appraised her niece carefully. "Very clever of you. But how do you t'ink you will stop the gossip about what the two of you were doing in that attic all night?"

"No one outside the family knows I was there." Jerralee's tone made it clear that she was confident the news would spread no further.

"This is a small town," Tante Olivette dismissed with an eloquent Acadian shrug. "Someone surely saw you leave, and they will talk."

"But it will only be *talk*. If I had called out for help, it would have been fact."

"*I* know you were there," Olivette said archly.

Jerralee sighed. "But you also know nothing happened."

"So you have told me. But I must wonder if you would recognize it if it had."

"*Tante*, that doesn't make sense. Of course I'd know."

"Did he not even try to kiss you?"

Jerralee smiled unwillingly at the memory of Nic's heated kisses.

Her aunt's eyes brightened. "He did, *non?* He kissed you."

Reluctantly, she nodded.

"Did you not kiss him back?" Olivette asked in an excited tone. When Jerralee didn't answer, she smiled knowingly. "Of course you did. He is a handsome devil, *non?*"

"I guess he's passably attractive if you like the haughty, aristocratic type," Jerralee allowed.

Tante Olivette folded her arms across her scrawny bosom. "It is as I had hoped."

Jerralee shook her head at the hopelessness of her aunt's romantic notions. "This family has some very strange ideas—"

"Poo-yie!" Olivette smacked her cheek dramatically. "I forgot about the family. They're coming for a meeting and will be here any minute. If you did not show up, I was going to send them searching the swamp for you."

"Good. We have a lot to talk about. Nic won't cooperate, and I want to discuss suing him."

LeBeaus began arriving a few minutes later. Their ebullient greetings would have been more appropriate had Jerralee just returned from a long exile in a hostile land. They were certainly relieved that she had been restored unharmed to the bosom of the family. But she suspected that much of their happiness stemmed from the fact that the annual softball game between the sugar mill and the flyswatter factory would not have to be postponed while they searched the swamp.

The meeting had scarcely begun when someone made the motion not to sue Nic. It was seconded and carried faster than any in the history of LeBeau family meetings. It was a warm summer day and everyone had softball—not business—on their minds. Jerralee cursed majority rule when the meeting adjourned despite her protests.

She didn't begrudge the family their ball game; she was a player and a fan herself. It was just that her relatives were showing signs of giving up on the craft guild completely. Many of them seemed content to leave things as they were, to work for Nic Delarue for the rest of their lives and retire on comfortable little pensions.

Hercule refused to go against their wishes by speaking to Nic on her behalf. As he so eloquently put it, "If you have a bone to pick with M'sieu Nic, you must do your own picking."

It was a job she did not look forward to.

The weather was hot and humid, a typically sweltering Louisiana day on which only true natives would even consider physical exertion. The two teams—the Millers and the Swatters—were evenly matched and the game was close, but Jerralee could think of little else but Nic as she moped on the sidelines. The last few days had been peculiar ones, and she wasn't sure why she felt so unraveled around him.

Maybe it was because he held the key to the realization of her dreams and she was reluctant to let anyone have that much control over her happiness. Whatever the reason for her discomfiture was, she was determined to put Nic Delarue out of her mind and concentrate on business.

She had thought long and hard about the craft guild and knew it would work. Once Sweetwood was restored and filled with live music and authentic Cajun cuisine, the tourists would come and they would buy the local crafts. The much-needed revenue would help all of Poulee Crossing. Other businesses would prosper and jobs would be created. It was a noble cause. So why was she the only person who seemed to understand how important it was?

Her reverie was interrupted when the buzzing sugar mill crowd suddenly fell silent. Jerralee looked up and tugged down the brim of her billed baseball cap to shade her eyes from the bright sunshine. Nic Delarue had arrived and was soliciting help to unload coolers of icy soft drinks and cold beer from his car. His unexpected appearance baffled the bystanders, and it was several uncomfortable moments before volunteers stepped forward.

Nic surveyed the surprised faces around him and smiled encouragingly. Everyone seemed ill at ease, and he hoped he hadn't made a mistake by coming here today. Even though he'd never attended the annual softball game before, he had decided it was time to open up communications between himself and the townspeople. He'd thought the game would be a good place to start.

Murmured greetings, strained but sincere, welcomed him. A couple of young men in orange sugar mill team shirts hefted the coolers and deposited them near the players' bench. Hoping his generosity would be accepted in the spirit it was offered, Nic announced that there would be hot dogs in the park for everyone after the game. He sighed with relief when the crowd cheered appreciatively.

Jerralee frowned at Nic. Evidently, noblesse oblige knew no bounds. She seethed when one of her cousins clapped Nic tentatively on the back. "Thank you, M'sieu Nic. You are a generous man."

He could afford to be generous when it came to hot dogs and beer. But ask for anything more and he wouldn't be so accommodating. She turned away in disgust when he began working the crowd like a mayoral candidate. He'd seemed hesitant at first, but it hadn't taken long for the Delarue charisma to kick in. What was he hoping to accomplish with such unprecedented and unnecessary friendliness? She was sure he had his reasons.

"M'sieu Nic," a pretty, teenaged girl on the sugar mill team called out softly. "Won't you play with us? We've heard you were quite a pitcher in your younger days."

Nic was not surprised that his athletic reputation had been discussed among the townspeople. In Poulee Crossing, where nothing truly exciting ever happened, any topic was fair game. "That was a long time ago," he demurred. "I'm not sure—"

"Come now, M'sieu Nic," Tante Olivette chimed in with a dozen others urging him to play. "Albert's bursitis is acting up and he can't pitch so good. We need you."

Olivette's words warmed Nic. It had been a long time since he'd heard them from anyone, and he'd forgotten how good it felt to be needed. "Well, if you really need me, perhaps I could pitch an inning."

Jerralee spun around and stalked away when she heard that. She was a fair pitcher herself and no one had asked *her* to play for the Millers. She sauntered over to the flyswatter group and struck up a conversation with the team captain, a man with whom she had once had a blind date.

"Cal, I'd be happy to pitch for your team if you want," she said with a flirtatious smile.

"The name's Claude," he answered with a good-natured grin. "Perhaps you forgot."

"Sorry." She smiled engagingly. "How about it?"

"I don't know," he said truthfully. "All your kin is on the other side. The Swatters might question your loyalty."

"I don't owe Delarue Sugar anything, you know that."

Claude nodded. It was well known that Jerralee was opposed to her family working for the sugar mill.

She shrugged. "It's your decision. So far the game is tied two and two. But your pitcher is looking pretty tired."

Claude pondered the situation. "Are you any good?"

"As good as Nic Delarue," she responded without false modesty.

"*C'est* okay, get out there and warm up that arm."

It had been a good idea to pit her skills against Nic's: it wouldn't hurt to remind him that she was his equal in all things. For two innings Jerralee pitched flawlessly, demonstrating outstanding athletic ability. Whenever she struck a Miller out, she glanced to Nic to make sure he had noticed. Maddeningly enough, he only smiled.

In the bottom of the fifth she threw him out when he attempted to steal second base. The Swatters were ahead four to three and her competitive spirit was honed. She was also getting a little cocky, and it showed.

Nic was disgusted with himself for making the team's third out. He yanked off his cap and slapped it against his thigh. When he looked up he saw Jerralee watching him with a smug look on her face. Determined not to let his impatience show, he made a sweeping gesture and bowed at the waist.

"I had no idea you had eyes in the back of your head," he called out as he marched up to the pitcher's mound to take her place.

"As I told you before, you don't know anything about me. Historically, Delarues have always underestimated the power of LeBeaus," she replied with a sly grin.

Jerralee was wearing white shorts and Nic couldn't take his eyes off her long, tanned legs as she walked to the bench. He felt that old familiar warmth rising inside him, but refused to admit that it was desire. Lust maybe, but not desire. Someone had given her a red team T-shirt emblazoned across the back with a gold flyswatter, but even the baggy garment could not conceal her shapely figure and he recalled how soft she had felt in his arms, how right their embrace had seemed.

As she sat down with the other team, Nic wondered why she had chosen to oppose the rest of the LeBeaus. It wasn't like her at all. Jerralee's idea of family unity made even the Three Musketeers' "all for one, one for all" ideology seem self-serving.

There could only be one explanation. She'd rather play against her own kin than be on the same team with him. He had tried to figure it out, but Nic still could not understand why Jerralee disliked him so much. He'd made enemies before, but none with quite the degree of unreasonableness as hers. He'd done nothing himself to deserve it, so he assumed the enmity she'd felt for the Delarues for so long had become a habit. But habits could be broken, and he made up his mind to be the one who would break hers.

What confused him the most was the way she responded to him. When they kissed, her body and her mind communed with his completely. When they got near each other, a powerful magic drew them together.

Maybe that was it. Maybe she wouldn't let herself get too close for fear she might have to acknowledge her own desire. In that case, he felt obliged to force her hand if necessary. And to show her that they were equals in all things. There would be no more Mister Nice Guy. If Jerralee wanted to play literal and figurative hardball, he was willing to give her a run for her money.

The Millers managed to keep the Swatters from scoring during the next inning. Dusk was making shadows among the live oaks in the park when they finally took their turn at bat. The rotund Hercule LeBeau surprised everyone by scoring an unbelievable home run, again tying the score. The hefty lawyer blasted the ball into the nearby bayou with a splat and huffed his way around the bases without even breaking a sweat.

Nic glanced at Jerralee and saw her cheer her cousin across home plate. Obviously, team spirit was no match for family loyalty after all.

When extra innings failed to break the tie the team captains conferred at the pitcher's mound. They elected to call the game because it was getting too dark

to play on the unlighted field. Everyone, hot and
hungry as they were, cheered the decision.

Everyone except Jerralee. She wanted to continue
the game, at least until she had bested Nic Delarue.
Again she was outvoted.

Nic was also disgruntled about the tie. He'd wanted
so badly to win. Or maybe, he admitted to himself,
what he really wanted was to conquer Jerralee's fighting spirit. After all, to the victor belonged the spoils.

The teams collected their equipment, and everyone
moved to the picnic area in the park adjacent to the
baseball diamond. The tie game had no losers, and
both players and spectators were in a jovial mood.
Backs were slapped, jokes were told and robust
laughter punctuated the shrill night music of trilling
tree frogs and chirping cicadas.

Zareh arrived with the food and started cooking,
but it was dark by the time the hot dogs were grilled.
Albert LeBeau produced a couple of kerosene lanterns for the serving area and bright moonlight suf-
ficed for everyone else.

In an effort to avoid Nic, Jerralee volunteered to
make the coffee. Soft drinks were fine for the children and the beer would be imbibed later, but the
adults wanted coffee with their meal. The dark roast
Zareh had provided was ground fine for dripping and
contained twenty percent chicory.

Jerralee had learned the art of coffee making as a
young girl, and performed the task with pride. For
each cup she placed a tablespoon of coffee in the
strainer of the drip pot balanced on the grate above the
hot coals of a firepit. Very slowly, she dripped boiling
water through the grounds, a spoonful at a time. She

watched it carefully, for once dripped, good Cajun coffee was never allowed to boil.

A deep voice behind her chanted an old Creole adage:

> Noir comme le Diable,
> Forte comme la mort,
> Doux comme l'amour,
> Chaud comme l'enfer!

Jerralee spun around and found herself almost in Nic Delarue's arms.

"Black as the devil, strong as death, sweet as love, hot as Hell!" he translated with a smile. "We Creoles are as passionate about our coffee as we are about other things."

"I wouldn't know about that," she said airily as she poured for the Swatters' shortstop.

Food plate in hand, Nic waited his turn and accepted a disposable cup of hot coffee. "You pitched a good game. You certainly are a woman of many talents."

"Thank you," she responded, her tone polite but formal.

"I wonder if I will ever truly know just how talented you are," he mused.

"The next time you need a small appliance repaired or a boat engine overhauled, give me a call. Now step along, Delarue, you're holding up the line."

Someone cleared his throat behind Nic and he walked away with a quick glance at Jerralee. She had returned the oversized T-shirt and now wore a pink cotton blouse with her shorts. The moonlight shimmered in her lustrous blond hair. It had been pulled up in an off-center ponytail that gave her an endearingly rakish air.

She was without a doubt the most unusual woman he had ever met. The most intriguing—and the most unapproachable. Never had he had so much trouble winning over a woman as he'd had winning over Jerralee LeBeau.

She had a one-track mind, and at the moment it happened to be set on restoring Sweetwood. He thought she was setting herself up for disappointment, but if she was determined to try, he knew he could help her. If only she would let him.

After loading a paper plate with hot dogs and chips, Jerralee walked over to the bleachers, sat down backward on one of the seats, and used the next row up as a makeshift table.

Claude followed and sat down beside her. "I didn't see your truck in the parking lot, Jerralee," he commented. "If you want, I'll take you home."

She was about to refuse when Nic, accompanied by dark-eyed Babette Bouchet, joined them. A flicker of something, which felt alarmingly like jealousy, made Jerralee reckless. "Why, thank you, Claude. I came with Tante Olivette, but she'll probably leave soon and I'm having much too much fun to go home early."

Claude frowned at the couple who'd joined them and Jerralee recalled that he and Babette had been courting for several months. He flashed Jerralee a wide smile and she decided she must have been mistaken about his relationship with the girl.

"We can take the long way," Claude whispered, just loud enough for Nic and Babette to overhear. "We can have even more fun than we can here."

Knowing Claude was using her to make Babette jealous, Jerralee scooted away from him and smiled at the brunette. She purposefully ignored Nic's presence. "Hello, Babette."

"Hello." The girl gave Claude a sideways glance. Nic nudged her onto the bleachers and they sat down facing Claude and Jerralee, their plates balancing precariously on their knees.

Nic spoke to Claude. "I'm afraid Miss LeBeau has forgotten that we have business to discuss tonight."

Jerralee feigned surprise. "Oh really? I thought our discussion was finished as far as you were concerned."

Nic smiled. "I wouldn't dream of disrupting the rest of your evening, but this is the only night I have free for a while," he said meaningfully, then turned his attention to the other man. "I believe you and Babette know each other, don't you, Claude?"

He nodded, then stared up into the starry sky with a pained expression on his face. "We do."

Babette sat her plate on the seat beside her and stood abruptly. "Excuse me, I have to go now." She darted down the bleachers and into the park.

Nic started to follow her, but Claude was already on his feet. "I'll take care of it."

Jerralee watched him sprint across the diamond toward the trees that bordered the park. She turned to Nic. "You really get a kick out of flaunting your power, don't you?"

"What are you talking about?"

"First you bring your girl over here, then you make up that lie about you and me having business to discuss. Not to mention the fact that you managed to get rid of Claude by sending him after your girlfriend."

"She's not my girlfriend," Nic told her. "She's Claude's almost-fiancée. Or at least she was until you batted those big blue eyes at him."

Jerralee tried to explain. "*He* followed *me.*"

"And why not? Every man in town considers you the greatest challenge of the decade. It would be a boost to any man's ego to win your heart. But what that fool of a boy doesn't know is that you are heartless, like most females."

"You have no right to accuse me of being unfeeling." Jerralee was on her feet by this time, her relish-laden hot dog in hand. Filled with indignation, she snapped, "I didn't know they were practically engaged."

Oblivious to the crowd gathering around them, Nic stood up and faced her down. "Everyone else in town knew it." He laughed without amusement. "Of course you're too wrapped up in your own selfish motives to see beyond your perky little nose."

Giving in to her passionate anger and all the other sensations that roiled inside her, Jerralee hauled back and threw the hot dog at Nic. She didn't run away as would have been prudent, but waited for his reaction. She didn't know what he would do, but after brushing at the relish staining his shirt, he pulled her into his arms for a rousing kiss—a form of retaliation that hadn't even crossed her mind.

Her lips burned beneath the warmth of his and she felt her anger melting, turning into something that she had no control over. She lifted her arms and wrapped them around his neck in an effort to get closer, but the laughter, catcalls and applause in the background broke her trance. She pushed away from him.

"Don't you ever do that again," she screeched.

"You repeat yourself, *cher*," he drawled. "If you can't take the heat, don't fan the flames."

Jerralee pushed past him and walked all the way home.

Tante Olivette was waiting for her on the front porch. She was shelling a pan of black-eyed peas and the steady *snap, snap, snap,* was loud in the silence. "What is going on between you and Nic Delarue, Minette?"

"Nothing," Jerralee grumbled, her anger having dissipated on the way home. "And we've already had this discussion once today."

"That was one magnificent kiss, Minette. Never have I seen such a kiss."

"It was nothing."

Olivette cackled with glee. "Not'ing, you say? Hah! I saw your reaction. It was somet'ing, all right. If this means what I t'ink—"

Jerralee reached into the pan and took out a hand-ful of peas to shell. "It doesn't!"

"Would you lie to your old *tante, cher?* I am not so old that I don't recognize passion when I see it."

"That's all it is, all it could ever be. He's an expe-rienced man and knows all the right moves. I'll admit I kissed him back. So what?"

"So maybe you might be falling in love with him, that's what is so."

Snap, snap, snap. A few more peas fell into the pan.

"Never."

"Why not, *cher?* He's handsome, rich and he's a good man."

"He's a Delarue."

"Posh," Olivette clucked. "Is that all?"

"You're not forgetting that our families have feuded for generations, are you?"

"That was then, this is now. It's time to end that foolishness."

"How can you say that when it's Nic who stands between us and the craft guild? Maybe you can forget that the guild is our last hope for the family to wriggle out from under Delarue control, but I can't. It's up to me to change things, don't you see?"

"Why do t'ings need to be changed? T'ings are not so bad."

"The family was cheated. Nic has all the land that should have been ours."

"Who in the family is unhappy with his lot in life?" Olivette wanted to know. "None of us are homeless, none are hungry, there is nothing we need that we cannot get."

"They don't know any different."

"We don't care to, *cher,*" Olivette said gently. "We're all satisfied. You are the only one of us who would change anyt'ing. I think you need a husband. It would give you somet'ing to do with all that energy of yours."

Jerralee rested her head in her hands. "Is that your answer to all the world's ills? Get Jerralee a husband?"

"It would be a start," the older woman said gravely.

"A husband would change nothing," Jerralee said as she got up to go in the house.

Tante Olivette smiled in the darkness. "The right one would."

Nic left the park soon after Jerralee and thought about her all the way home to Long Shadows. Assuming he was alone in the house, he plopped down in one of the chairs in his study with a glass of brandy. He looked up in surprise when Zareh spoke behind him.

"I go now, M'sieu Nic."

"Before you do, I want to talk to you." Nic set his brandy snifter down on the table. "What have you done, Zareh?"

"Done? *Moi?*" she asked innocently.

"You know perfectly well what I'm talking about. Did you make any potions? Sprinkle any ashes? Chant any incantation? What have you done?"

"I cast no spells, M'sieu Nic. Did you not advise against it?"

"I did. But you locked the attic door on purpose that night."

"To everyt'ing there is a purpose, but I cast no spells," she repeated adamantly.

"Then why can't I resist her when I want to so badly?" he demanded. "Why can't I get that infernal woman out of my mind?"

"Jerralee LeBeau?" she asked as if she didn't know.

"That's the one," he said sarcastically. "Tonight when she threw that hot dog at me, I wanted to smack her. The next thing I knew I was kissing her. Dammit, I want to know what's happening to me."

"Perhaps she is working her magic on you, M'sieu Nic."

"She has the power to do that?" he asked, disbelieving.

"*Oui*. All women have that power with the right man and all men have it with the right woman. It is the strongest magic of all. Love."

He should have know better than to bandy words about with Zareh; she'd never admit it even if she had interfered by casting a spell over him. It didn't matter. He didn't believe in magic and he didn't really believe in love, either. "Never mind, Zareh. But no more hocus-pocus."

"I assure you, M'sieu Nic, I have cast no spells and I will cast none." Zareh's bangles jingled as she left the house.

Nic wanted to believe her, but what else would explain the crazy attraction he felt for a woman who despised him? But did she despise him? For someone who had thrown a hot dog at him, Jerralee had seemed more than willing to follow his lead until the noise from the crowd had interrupted their kiss.

Nic downed the brandy, poured another glass and took it into his bedroom. He undressed and stepped into the shower, but the cool water failed to ease his mind or his body. He kept wondering how far things might have gone if they had been alone tonight.

Determined to forget about her for a few hours, he climbed into bed, relaxed against the pillows and gulped his second brandy. Feeling somewhat refreshed and soothed, he felt himself drifting into sleep. Then the phone rang.

"Hello," he answered in a sleep-husky voice.

"Nic, this is Jerralee LeBeau."

"Why are you whispering?"

"Because I don't want anyone to know I'm calling you."

"What can I do for you?"

"I want to ask you something."

"Ask away."

"Did you mean it?"

For a moment he thought she might be referring to the kiss. If so, he'd never meant anything more. "I meant it."

"Then you are willing to talk business with me?"

"What?"

"That's what you said earlier tonight."

"I was just trying to get Claude out of your clutches before Babette's father fetched his shotgun."

"They eloped tonight."

"How do you know that?"

"Althea Nooley just called Tante Olivette with the news. So, you really had no intention of talking business with me tonight?"

"I'm in bed, Jerralee."

"So am I, but I wanted to give you one last chance."

"To do what?"

"Talk about settling things between us."

Nic wanted nothing more than to do just that. If the only way he could get her out of his life and off his mind was to meet with her, he would risk it. "Your place or mine?"

"Neither. And not now. How about tomorrow?"

"I'll be in Baton Rouge for the next two days."

"Perfect. I'll meet you there for lunch tomorrow."

"You're willing to go all the way to Baton Rouge just to have lunch with me? Should I be flattered?"

"No. But that way no one will know we're meeting."

He sighed. "I don't know what you want."

"I'll explain it over lunch." She named a poor boy sandwich shop and gave him the location.

"I've never heard of the place."

"Neither has anyone else in Poulee Crossing. I'll meet you there at twelve o'clock."

Because he didn't want her to think she could always have her way with him, he grinned and said, "Better make it one o'clock instead."

Chapter Seven

Jerralee put on an unheard-of amount of makeup and changed clothes in a service station rest room. She'd left Poulee Crossing in work clothes, but knew she needed a disguise for her lunch with Nic. As she surveyed herself in the grimy mirror, she decided that no one would recognize her in this getup. Not even Nic.

An impatient patron pounded on the door.

"I'll be out in a moment," she called as she wiggled into a pair of silk panty hose. She slipped the red dress she'd secretly borrowed from her cousin Deidre over her head and squirmed to pull up the zipper. She fluffed out her hair and perched a straw hat with a red ribbon on her head. She dug a pair of oversized sunglasses out of her bag and put them on.

The pounding on the door began again and an irate

voice called out, "Hurry up, will you? You've been in there long enough."

Jerralee eased her feet into a pair of high-heeled sandals, rolled her sneakers into her shirt and jeans and tucked the bundle into a straw tote bag. Another glance in the mirror gave her the needed confidence that she wouldn't be recognized and she flung open the door.

"It's about time," said the waiting young woman. She was holding the hand of a little girl who was hopping about at her side.

"I'm sorry I took so long," Jerralee apologized as she hurried to her truck. But when she turned the key in the ignition all she got was a metallic grating sound. She groaned. Please, not now. She had taken so much time changing that she was running late and couldn't afford any more delays. She jumped out of the truck and popped open the hood.

The station attendant stepped up beside her. "Need some help, lady?"

"It's the starter. It's been trying to go out on me for a week now."

The middle-aged man peered over her shoulder into the innards of the truck. "Sure sounded like the starter."

"I need a new one. Can you fix it for me today?"

"I'll have to get the part and it'll take a couple of hours."

Jerralee hated paying for an expensive repair job that she could easily do herself, but there were more important matters at stake here. "Do it. I'll take a cab and come back for it later."

* * *

Nic had been waiting in the sandwich shop for over half an hour. Deciding he'd been stood up, he finished the soft drink he'd ordered and left. He'd just stepped out onto the sidewalk when a cab screeched into the parking lot off Seigen Lane and Jerralee stepped out.

At least he thought it was Jerralee. But he couldn't be sure since he'd never seen her so dressed up before. The silky dress she wore clung to her curves and showed off her figure to perfection.

He smiled as an errant breeze lifted the full skirt of her dress. It was definitely Jerralee. He'd recognize those gorgeous legs anywhere.

"Sorry I'm late," she called breathlessly as she paid off the cabby. "Do you have another appointment?" She hurried up to him, holding her floppy hat on her head with one hand and an oversized bag in the other.

"No," he lied, knowing that he could put the bank officers off until tomorrow. He could conduct business anytime, but it wasn't everyday he had a chance to give Jerralee a taste of life outside Poulee Crossing. He dismissed the sandwich shop with a wave.

"We're not having lunch here, we're going to Mulate's."

He took her arm and guided her down the street where he'd parked his car, a sleek import.

"What's wrong with the restaurant I chose?" she wanted to know.

"Nothing. It's a fine restaurant for people in a hurry. But I plan to linger over my lunch and I want it to be worth lingering over."

"Oh." Jerralee knew Mulate's only by reputation, since it was billed in advertisements as the world's most famous Cajun restaurant. No doubt the food was superior to that of the sandwich shop's, but she had picked that place specifically because of its unromantic atmosphere. Mulate's was another story.

Things weren't working out as she'd planned and, as usual when she was with Nic, Jerralee felt out of control. She couldn't relax and the tension building inside her was rather like the kind experienced during a roller coaster ride. She knew something exciting could happen at any moment, but she didn't know exactly what or when.

Nic drove west on Perkins Road, then turned onto Bluebonnet, where Mulate's Restaurant was located. He parked and switched off the engine.

"Don't move," he warned ominously. Then he got out of the car and walked around to her door.

"I can open my own door," she told him as he performed the task for her.

"I know. But when you're with me, I'll do it."

He took her arm and escorted her into the restaurant. A smiling hostess, who seemed to know him, showed them to a secluded corner table covered with a red-and-white checked tablecloth. As Nic pulled out her chair Jerralee noticed that thousands of business cards decorated a ceiling supported by strategically placed cypress beams.

The wall behind the bandstand was adorned with bronzed shoes and she wondered if any of them had been worn out on the wooden dance floor, dancing to the lively zydeco music.

An alligator skin was hung from the ceiling directly above the dance floor, and the other walls were decorated with paintings of swamp scenes and colorful festival posters.

Nic watched Jerralee take in her surroundings. "Have you ever been here before?"

"No."

A young waiter wearing a silky red shirt and tight black pants stepped up to the table in time to hear Jerralee's reply. "Then I would suggest the veal grillades. The chef browns the meat delicately before simmering it in a browned tomato sauce. It's served over rice and it's delicious."

"Very well," she said as she handed the menu back to the waiter. "I'll try it."

Nic ordered the same. As the waiter turned away the band struck up a lively tune, the accordion and banjos giving it a distinctive Cajun sound. Nic stood up and held out his hand. "Come waltz with me."

The restaurant lighting was dim and Jerralee had taken off her sunglasses to read the menu. Glancing around nervously, she put them back on and shook her head.

"No one from Poulee Crossing is here to recognize you." Nic leaned over, removed her glasses and tossed them onto the table. Taking her hand, he pulled her to her feet. "Come on, just one little dance, *cher*."

She followed him reluctantly onto the floor. "I didn't come here to dance, I came here to talk business with you."

"And I promise we will," he said, as he swept her into his arms. "But I talk business all the time, and I seldom have a chance to dance with such a beautiful woman.''

Nic was light on his feet and he twirled her around the floor gracefully. There was a maddening hint of arrogance about him that aroused her and made her body ache for a greater closeness.

He smiled down at her. Staring into her eyes, he took her hands in his and pulled her against him. His heart thudded in cadence to her own. Then he pushed her away again, whirling her around and around, before finally returning her to his embrace.

Jerralee laughed with delight. "Not so fast, you're making me dizzy."

"I feel a little dizzy, myself." He grinned. "Fun, isn't it?"

"Yes," she admitted breathlessly. They danced several more dances, and she was sorry when their lunch arrived and they had to sit down.

Between the zestful atmosphere and the delicious Cajun food, Jerralee found herself relaxing enough to tell Nic her plans for Sweetwood. She explained that, while other economically depressed areas struggled to attract the high technology firms, she wanted to take the opposite approach and focus on low-tech hand-crafts.

She detailed how she wanted to restore the plantation house to its former splendor and use the refurbished rooms to showcase the skills of local artisans. By serving authentic Cajun food and providing a background of foot-stomping music, she hoped to attract tourists on their way to the larger cities.

Nic was enthusiastic about her ideas and gave her a few of his own. At last they had found something to discuss that did not result in dissension, and when he suggested that they take a drive along the River Road after the two-hour lunch, she agreed.

"The name Baton Rouge reminds me of us," Nic remarked as he drove. The sunroof was open and the distinctive smell of the Mississippi River drifted into the car.

"I never thought of it that way, but you're right. It reputedly refers to the red stick that marked the boundary between two feuding Indian tribes." Somehow the day seemed a little less bright after she had been reminded of the invisible wall that stood between her and Nic.

They drove past the State Capitol, a thirty-four story art deco building that was also the tallest capitol in the country. Its observation deck looked out over the Mississippi River for three miles in either direction.

"So you hope to restore Sweetwood with the money from the IOU, if it's valid," Nic said as he turned north onto Highway 61.

"That's the plan," she agreed.

"Then we should visit the Fantôme Maison Plantation. I'll bet you've never been inside, have you?"

"No, and I really don't have time today. I still have to get my truck and drive back to Poulee Crossing."

"Nonsense, it's only a little after three o'clock. We'll be back in a couple of hours."

"That mean's I'll be late for supper and I told Tante Olivette I'd be there."

He glanced at her and smiled. "Live dangerously for once. Call her and tell her you've had a change of plans. Fantôme Maison belongs to a friend of mine and if he's there I'm sure he'll be happy to give you some advice about restoring a plantation house. Of course, it has something that Sweetwood will never have."

"What's that?"

"Ghosts. It's haunted."

Jerralee frowned. She didn't want to give her aunt any encouragement when it came to Nic Delarue. But she would like to talk to the owner of a restored plantation house, haunted or not. A trip to Fantôme Maison could be inspiring. She could see what Sweetwood might be like if things worked out the way she hoped.

"It's all in the name of business," he pointed out.

"I know."

He pulled into a convenience store parking lot and stopped near a pay telephone. "Make up your mind. Are you game?"

"Yes," she said impulsively as she got out of the car to make the phone call. It seemed she was always acting impulsively these days.

Nic told her about his childhood at Long Shadows as he drove to Fantôme Maison. His mother had died when he was young and Zareh Dulac had been a surrogate mother to him. He had never made friends among the local children because his father had seen fit to enroll him in only the best private schools.

"You know," Jerralee told him when he'd finished his story, "you're the only person I know who rode to school every day in a chauffeured Cadillac."

"And you are the only person I know who has a pet alligator."

A long, wide driveway curved between spreading live oaks dripping with Spanish moss and led to the white-columned house known as Fantôme Maison. The Greek Revival mansion was surrounded by a lush paradise of flowering magnolia and stately poplars. Tropical flowers bloomed in colorful profusion in beds scattered about on the manicured grounds.

When Jerralee stepped out of the car, the air was heavy with the sweet scent of honeysuckle and wild jasmine. Sunlight filtered gently through the trees and traced shadows on the walk that led up to the house. The ivy-draped columns supported a deep, sloping roof. Inside, the foyer was floored in marble, and a sweeping mahogany staircase led up to a white wrought-iron balcony circling the second and third floors.

The hostess who greeted them at the door recognized Nic at once. "Mr. Delarue, how nice to see you again. I'm sorry to say that Mr. St. Pierre isn't in and isn't expected back today. Is there anything I can do for you?"

Nic introduced the two women. "Marcus wasn't expecting me, Celine. I just happened to be in town and thought I'd bring Mademoiselle LeBeau out for a tour."

"The guides are already taken, but I can accompany you myself, if you'd like."

"I don't want to take you from your duties," Nic said. "I think I know the legends well enough to do them justice."

As they walked up the stairs Nic told Jerralee some of the house's history. "Fantôme Maison was built in the late 1700s by the St. Pierre family. Originally each floor had four rooms, but in the mid 1800s extra rooms were added to the ground floor."

As Jerralee ran her hand along the banister a shiver ran up her spine. "*Fantôme* is French for phantom or ghost. Has it always been haunted?"

"In the beginning it was simply know as Maison St. Pierre. In 1854 Valaine St. Pierre and Maria Castillo fell madly in love, but their families were bitter enemies. They took matters into their own hands and eloped, thinking that in time their relatives would come to accept their marriage."

Jerralee knew this was not a new story in the region. The Spanish and French had always had their differences. Baton Rouge was one of the earliest French settlements in Louisiana. However, it had been under Spanish control in 1779, and later, in 1810, had come under American control.

"But their families couldn't overlook their respective backgrounds for a little thing like 'true love,'" she surmised. "Let me guess. Valaine and Maria came to a tragic end?"

Nic smiled enigmatically. "Very tragic." He opened a beautifully detailed handcarved door. "A short six months after they were married Maria gave birth to twin sons in that very bed."

Jerralee stepped into the bedroom. The walls were covered with blue watered silk, which matched the silk bed draperies. The oak floor was polished to a high gloss and covered with an antique Axminster carpet in a soft silver color. The bedroom furniture was made of burled walnut, and a pair of Chippendale chairs with needlepoint cushions stood near the window.

"It's a beautiful room," Jerralee said. She glanced at the massive bed hung with silk draperies and thought about the twin babies who had been born there. "The births did not please either family," she guessed.

Nic nodded. "Maria's mother took to her bed and her father disowned her, but her brother Eduardo was livid. He stormed the house and demanded satisfaction."

"A duel?"

Nic stepped over to a bedside table and opened a drawer. He withdrew a carved teakwood box.

"Yes, but Eduardo knew Valaine was the better shot, so he sought to even the odds by turning to fire before the count was finished. Maria, seeing that her brother meant to murder her husband, stepped into the line of fire in an effort to reason with him. Maria and Valaine were killed with the same bullet, shot from one of these pistols."

He opened the box. A pair of silver-handled dueling pistols rested on a bed of velvet inside.

Jerralee shuddered at the sight of the weapons and closed the box. "What happened to the babies?"

"Valaine's widowed sister moved in to rear them."

"Didn't the Castillo family have anything to say about their grandchildren?"

Nic shrugged. "It's rumored they went back to Spain in disgrace and were never heard from again."

"Then I take it Maria and Valaine are the resident ghosts?"

"After all the hostilities, they could hardly allow their offspring to be raised by either family without keeping a watchful eye. The twins were wild and unrestrained as youngsters and it has been said that they escaped injury at the last possible moment from hundreds of close calls."

"Maria and Valaine?" she asked.

"Their *tante* first claimed it was a result of black magic worked by one of the family's slaves. Then a visit by the apparitions of her brother and sister-in-law made a believer out of her. She lived to a ripe old age and was fond of repeating the stories to all who would listen."

Down the hall in the well-appointed nursery Jerralee was drawn to a delicate music box on a bureau. It was made of pewter in the shape of a heart and had a filigreed pattern of lovebirds on the cover. When she lifted the top the haunting strains of an old French lullaby filled the room.

Hairs lifted at her nape and she felt a strange presence. She turned quickly, expecting to find a ghostly stranger in the room. There was no one there but Nic.

"I always feel restless in here," he said softly.

"Do you come here often?"

"Not so much anymore. Marcus and I went to the same school and virtually grew up together. His grandfather lived in the house then. I've been here many times, but we were never allowed to touch anything in the nursery, lest we summon the family phantoms."

Jerralee snapped the lid on the music box closed. "But the twins were all right, weren't they? Don't tell me something bad happened to them."

"They were fine," he assured her. "They both lived to be ninety-four and died within a few hours of each other. One of them was Marcus's great-grandfather."

"Is Marcus the sole owner now?"

"Yes, he's the oldest male heir, and everything will go to his son. Marcus lived here himself until a few years ago, but the place finally got to his wife. After the birth of their baby Jeanne complained about interference from the ghosts.''

"What kind of interference?" Jerralee asked with a superstitious shiver.

"Harmless things. Sometimes, if the night turned chilly, Jeanne would get up to cover the baby and find that someone had already tucked him in. Other times she would hear the baby crying, but by the time she got to his room he had stopped because the cradle was rocking gently by itself.''

"That's spooky.''

"Yes, it is," he agreed. "But interesting. It's too bad Sweetwood isn't haunted. It's a great draw for tourists.''

She grinned. "Maybe we could advertise. 'Wanted for hire: old ghosts with colorful histories. Only those with haunting experience need apply.'''

"That's a good idea," he agreed. "It's paid off for Fantôme Maison.''

"Why did Marcus decide to open it to the public?"

"When he and Jeanne moved into town to a nice, quiet townhouse, he couldn't bear the thought of selling it. He hoped to make it profitable."

"And is it?" she asked.

"Not according to Marcus. It's a popular spot for tourists, but it costs so much to maintain that it barely breaks even. But he wants to keep it in the family." Nic shrugged. "He's a rich man, he can afford to be sentimental about such things.''

He continued the tour and the more Jerralee saw of Fantôme Maison, the more she realized what a pipe dream restoring Sweetwood really was. Eighteen thousand dollars was a drop in the bucket compared to what would be needed to renovate her neglected family legacy. Even if the LeBeaus did most of the labor themselves, the supplies and period furnishings would cost five times what she hoped to win from Nic.

Was that why he had insisted on bringing her here? To point out the futility of her dreams?

"You're very quiet," Nic observed as they strolled down the gracious walk to the car.

Some of Jerralee's disappointment congealed into anger. "You did this on purpose, didn't you?"

"What?"

"You thought bringing me here and showing me what I'd be up against would make me give up on Sweetwood and the craft guild."

"I only thought to give you a taste of reality."

"And that is?"

"You cannot do it alone. Your ideas for the craft guild, as you outlined them over lunch, sound excellent, but you need strong financial backing."

What he said was true, but Jerralee was not prepared to admit defeat. "What I need is the money your family owes mine."

Nic sighed as he started the car's engine. "If you can prove to my satisfaction that I do indeed owe you eighteen thousand dollars, I will gladly write you a check. In the meantime, I'd appreciate it if you'd stop maligning my character."

"Fine. Now if you'll just be kind enough to take me back to Baton Rouge, I'll get a cab there and fetch my truck."

"Nonsense. I'll take you, where is it?"

"At a service station on Hooper Road. The mechanic should be finished with the repairs by now." She gave him directions and they rode the rest of the way in uneasy silence.

When Nic pulled into the station, it was evident that it was closed. Jerralee got out and peeked through the window of the service bay to find her truck locked inside. That did little to improve her temper.

"This is all your fault," she accused.

"Mine?" Nic stood up and leaned out of the sunroof.

"If you had brought me back when I asked you, I'd have been home by now."

"Okay then, I'll take you home."

"You can't do that!" Jerralee rolled her eyes toward heaven. "As it is, everyone in the parish is already speculating about us after the hot dog incident."

"Then I'll take you to a motel."

"Right. I have about eighty dollars in my purse, and I have to use that to get my truck out of hock tomorrow."

"I'll pay for the room. After all," he said sarcastically, "it's my fault that you're in this predicament."

"I'm not a charity case, you know. I make a darn good living."

"I don't recall belittling your occupation. But if your independence means so much to you, write a check or put it on a credit card."

"I didn't bring my checkbook and I don't believe in plastic money."

Nic shook his head in disbelief. "A woman without credit cards? That's like an octopus without arms."

"If you believe all women are alike, you're wrong. What did women ever do to you to make you so bitter?"

He looked at her intently, his wide brown eyes full of old pain. "They disappointed me," he said honestly. "But since you are a lifelong resident of Poulee Crossing, you no doubt are already familiar with my history."

When she said nothing more Nic sat down behind the wheel and pushed the electric window control. Once the glass was down, he said, "I'm going to my hotel. Do you want a ride or not?"

Jerralee stalked around to the passenger side, yanked open the door and plopped into the seat.

"I take that as an affirmative answer," he said before he sped away.

The ride to the hotel was coldly silent. When the parking valet opened Jerralee's door, Nic leaned close and whispered, "I'm going to get another room and have it put on my bill. If your conscience bothers you, you can send me a check later, but I don't want any scenes in the lobby. Understand?"

"I don't have any choice."

She crossed the opulent lobby and waited for Nic by the elevator, hoping she wouldn't see anyone she knew. Not that they would recognize her in the bright red dress, big hat and sunglasses. In fact, her attire might well make someone mistake her intentions and her occupation altogether.

Nic dealt with the desk clerk, and as they entered the elevator, he handed her a key.

"What floor are you on?" she asked, her finger poised above the number panel.

"Three."

Jerralee looked at her key card. "So am I."

"It's right next door, as a matter of fact. I didn't even notice until the clerk handed me the key."

"Why didn't you specify a room on another floor?"

"It would only have confirmed what he already suspected. I felt the less attention drawn to the matter, the better. If you want, I'll take the key back and—"

"No, I'll keep it." He was right, and it was difficult to stay mad at him when he was trying so hard to be obliging. As soon as the elevator doors opened, she marched down the hall in search of Room 314. Without even saying good-night, she escaped into the safety of her room.

The first thing Jerralee saw was the connecting door to what was evidently Nic's room. She placed her ear against it and heard him enter next door. He opened and closed a couple of drawers, then she heard the shower running.

It wasn't difficult to conjure up a mental picture of him in the shower when the memory of him in that scrap of a bathing suit was still imprinted on her mind. She turned on the television set to drown out the sound of the water, but the images on the screen couldn't compare with the ones in her head.

Nic let the cold water sluice over him. He'd taken more cold showers since he'd met Jerralee LeBeau than he had in his whole shower-taking life. He didn't want to think about her, so why was she always on his mind? Was it because of the challenge she represented? Or was it the fact that she was so damned un-attainable?

He towel-dried his hair, wrapped another towel around his waist and strode across the room to the connecting door. He knocked softly and, much to his surprise, she answered immediately.

"Yes?"

"Have you called your aunt to explain things?" he asked through the door.

Jerralee sighed. "I called, but I don't think she really believes this situation is as innocent as it is."

"Shall I corroborate your story?" he teased.

"Heavens, no," she gasped. "That would only make things worse."

"Have you ordered dinner?"

"No."

"Are you hungry?"

Jerralee wanted to tell him that she was a big girl, she could take care of herself, but somehow the words came out wrong. "A little."

"I hate eating alone and I thought that since we're both stuck here we might as well have dinner together."

When she didn't answer, he hastily added, "It wouldn't mean anything."

"I know," she said on a sigh. "After that lunch today, all I want is a sandwich."

Nic had changed out of his business suit after his shower into a casual shirt and trousers. Jerralee didn't have any fresh clothes, but she left the hat and sunglasses in her room. They walked to a small place near the hotel that served authentic Sicilian muffuletta sandwiches, made with layered Italian-style meats and cheeses and a unique olive salad in a round loaf of crusty bread.

Jerralee confessed that she was becoming disillusioned about the craft guild. "Seeing how much goes into restoring a house that size makes me doubt if I could ever get a restoration of Sweetwood off the ground."

"You could still do it," he told her. "At first, it would just have to be on a smaller scale than you've envisioned."

"But eighteen thousand dollars won't be nearly enough."

"That's true, but as you said, you and your relatives can do most of the work. You can save a lot of money that way. Have you considered applying for a Small Business Administration loan?"

"Do you think I could qualify?"

"I don't know. You could try." The light from the candle on the table reflected in Jerralee's eyes and Nic felt himself drawn into their cerulean depths.

"I might do that."

"I think the guild could ultimately benefit the whole community. Maybe even the whole parish."

"But we'd only have our spare time to devote to the project and it could take years to finish," she disparaged.

"You're not going anywhere, are you?"

"No."

"What's your primary goal in establishing the craft guild?" he asked.

"I want the family to be self-sufficient, so they don't have to depend on outside jobs."

"In other words," he said flatly. "You don't want them working for a Delarue."

"It's nothing personal." Jerralee sighed. "In fact as Delarues go, I must admit you're not so bad."

"Is that a compliment?"

"Let's call it an honest observation."

Nic's grin was easy. "And to think, I used to admire honesty in a woman."

"Tante Olivette says that if you can't be honest, be kind."

"I like your *tante*," Nic said. "In fact, I like all your relatives."

"They can be a bit intimidating at times."

"I understand they're trying to marry you off," he commented casually, wondering who they had in mind to undertake that pleasant but difficult task.

"Yes, they are. And don't be surprised if you turn out to be the talk of the parish when you get back to Poulee Crossing."

"Just because we happen to be in Baton Rouge at the same time?" he asked.

"Word will get out that we were together."

"How? No one saw us, and I promise not to tell."

"I told Tante Olivette I was here. She'll put four and four together and come up with ten."

"But you're her niece."

"Next to Althea Nooley, she's the worst gossip in the parish."

"Swear her to secrecy."

"I've already made her promise not to tell a living soul. Which will definitely limit the recipients of the story to her closest friends."

Nic laughed and they finished their dinner. They strolled slowly back to the hotel and paused outside Jerralee's room while she searched in her bag for her key card. She located it and when she looked up, caught Nic watching her intently.

Before she quite knew what was happening, he kissed her. A warm, lingering kiss filled with yearning. Yet the situation was too dangerous to allow herself to get carried away and Jerralee broke the embrace after several delicious moments.

"I had a good time today," she told him. "Thanks for showing me around."

"Do you like the city?" he asked.

"It's fun to visit, but Poulee Crossing is my home. I won't feel really comfortable until I get back there."

"We have more in common than you think, *cher.*" His lips descended again, but she stepped around him and unlocked the door.

"Today was a wonderful moment out of time, Nic. But you and I both know that there can never be anything more between us."

"And why is that?"

"Because you're a Delarue and I'm a LeBeau."

"That's not good enough anymore, *cher,*" he told her softly. "I've never had this kind of magic with anyone else."

"Neither have I," she admitted.

"Then how can you deny what is meant to be? Will you sacrifice our happiness because our ancestors started a feud?"

"I can't forget the past as easily as you can."

"And yet you can deny the feelings we have for each other?"

She ducked into her room. "We are opponents, Nic. We cannot be lovers, too."

Chapter Eight

Despite having spent a restless night thinking about Jerralee, Nic woke up feeling warm and happy the next morning. After hard thought and lengthy self-debate he'd come to an unsettling conclusion.

He was in love.

He hadn't wanted to fall in love. In fact, falling in love hadn't even been on his agenda. But since meeting that blue-eyed Cajun spitfire, he'd been set on a dizzying and inevitable course in that direction. He'd fought it as long as he could and he was tired of running away from his feelings. Jerralee LeBeau had come into his life and she was there to stay.

She made him feel alive and vital, and it had been a long time since he'd experienced the depth of emotion he felt with her. If indeed he ever had. Granted, sometimes the emotion she provoked was frustration. Sometimes it was ambivalence, sometimes plain shock. But whatever it was, it was powerful. He would never cease to be intrigued by her, and for the first time in years he thought seriously about his future. About a future with Jerralee.

Nic needed to hear her voice, to reaffirm the profound urgings of his heart. He rolled over in bed, reached for the phone and rung up her room.

After a dozen rings he hung up. To confirm his suspicion that she had already left town, he called the service station that had repaired her truck. The mechanic told him what he already knew: she had picked up the vehicle an hour ago and was on her way back to Poulee Crossing.

Nic slammed down the phone, adding anger to the list of strong emotions she instilled in him. He showered and shaved and got dressed for the business appointments that could not be postponed another day. He couldn't believe she had left without a word to him, especially at such a crucial point in their relationship. He would never understand her.

Nic checked out of the hotel and finished his Baton Rouge business in record time. When he returned to Long Shadows later in the afternoon, Zareh met him at the door with a happy grin on her face.

"Is is true, M'sieu Nic?"

"That's hard to answer, since I have no idea what you're talking about. Is what true?"

"It is all over town that you and Mam'selle Jerralee went to Baton Rouge together. Alistair Moncreif saw you leave a sandwich shop on Seigen Lane." Zareh flashed another beaming grin. "He said the two of you made a handsome couple."

"I don't even know Alistair Moncreif," Nic said with bewilderment.

"Oh, he is *cousin secondaire* to Ella Jenkins, who is neighbor to Penny Swope, who is best friend to Althea Nooley."

"Ah, yes, the infamous Althea Nooley." So someone had seen them. So what?

"Word travels fast—"

"In a small town," he finished for her. "I'd appreciate it if you would stop spreading gossip, Zareh." Now there was a hopeless request.

"I have spread not'ing, I have merely listened. Do you deny that you are having an affair with Mam'selle?"

"What I had with Mam'selle cannot be termed an affair. A tête-à-tête, perhaps, but definitely not an affair. We had lunch together, that's all."

"Her family says she did not come home all night, M'sieu. Their hearts are concerned for her honor."

"Her truck broke down and she stayed over until it was repaired."

Zareh clasped her hands together and smiled. "Always, I have known this day would come."

"No day has come. We did not stay together. There is nothing between Jerralee LeBeau and myself except a complete lack of understanding."

Zareh was crestfallen. "You mean there has been no—"

"None," he pronounced emphatically.

"*Mon Dieu!* Why not?"

"That, my nosey friend, is none of your business. Actually, none of this is your concern." He picked up his bag and started upstairs.

"You are angry with old Zareh, M'sieu Nic. All I have done, I have done for you," she called after him.

Nic stopped in his tracks. "What exactly have you done, Zareh?"

"Try not to be too angry with me. Remember that I promised your poor dying *maman* that I would always look after you," she reminded him.

"Zareh?"

"And remember that I want no more than to see you settled and happy."

"Zareh," he demanded a bit more firmly.

"I only thought to reverse the curse. That is why I did what I did."

Nic sagged against the banister. His worst suspicions were confirmed. He didn't want to believe in black magic, but a charm or spell would certainly explain the intense feelings he had for a wholly unsuitable woman. He should have been relieved that there was a perfectly illogical explanation for everything, but he wasn't.

"So," he sighed, as he retraced his steps down the stairs. "You're behind all this. The desire I feel for Jerralee isn't really a result of falling in love, it's just a by-product of your infernal voodoo."

"Ah," Zareh breathed. "So you are falling in love? Is that not wonderful?"

Nic went straight into his study and poured himself a stiff drink. Normally, he didn't touch the stuff before sunset, but he had no trouble downing it even at this time of day.

Zareh followed him uninvited. "What is wrong?"

Nic sloshed more brandy into the glass. "I want you to uncast the spell you've placed on me," he said with quiet urgency. "Immediately."

"Spell? I have cast no spells, M'sieu." Zareh looked confused. "I tol' you before that love creates its own magic."

Nic looked up in bewilderment. As devious as she was at times, Zareh would never lie to him. "Do you mean to tell me that my feelings haven't been influenced by hexes or potions or sprinklings of fairy dust?"

"Non."

Nic sank onto a chair. "Then maybe you'd better sit down and explain exactly what you have done."

Zareh took her time settling herself in a chair near his. "Nothing really so bad."

"It's been a long day and I'm losing patience, Zareh. Tell me."

"I brought Mam'selle to you and that was good." When he didn't answer, she added, *"Non?"*

"Just how did you accomplish that amazing feat?"

"Everyone in Poulee Crossing knows how that girl longs to restore her old homeplace. That is all she talks about. But everybody also know she don' have the money."

She glanced at Nic for confirmation of her facts.

"I'm listening."

"So, I made the IOU and slip' it into a box with her family's old papers."

"You did what?" he thundered.

"I find some old paper in the attic. I tear off a piece. I make up some ink. I scratch it out with a goose feather. Very easy."

"How did you manage to plant the thing in Jerralee's house?"

"It was embarrassingly simple. Nobody was home and I just walk' in. Someone should tell them people to lock their doors when they go out, *non?*"

Nic fell back in the chair and rubbed his temples. He had no idea what he was going to do now. If he confessed this bit of duplicity, Jerralee would probably have Zareh arrested for breaking and entering, and him shot for aiding and abetting.

When he woke up this morning things had seemed simple and straightforward. He loved Jerralee and he knew she loved him, too, or she wouldn't respond the way she did when he kissed her. The problem was *she* didn't know it yet.

When he'd left Baton Rouge this afternoon, he'd had every reason to believe that he might yet win her affections. It wouldn't be easy because of her inherent distrust of Delarues, but he'd hoped that by being open, honest and loving, he could change her mind.

Zareh's confession presented an impossible obstacle. If he told Jerralee what he'd learned, she'd think he was trying to get out of paying her by claiming the IOU was a fake. If he didn't tell her and she found out on her own, she would never believe in him.

"Who else knows about this, Zareh?"

"I tol' only you."

"Then we must keep this a secret between us."

"You will not tell Mam'selle? Do you think that wise?"

"Maybe not, but it's the only choice I have. I plan to marry her if she'll have me and I'm not willing to take any chances." He hadn't known he was marriage-minded, but now that he'd spoken the words, he realized they were true.

"What if she finds out?"

Nic shrugged that particular worry away. "Someday, when we've been married about ten or twenty years, I'll confess. We'll have a good laugh over it."

"But would it not be better to start out as you mean to go on? If she loves you, she will understand." Zareh asked softly, "She loves you, does she not?"

"If she doesn't already, she will by the time I'm finished," he said with more conviction than he felt.

"You will win her, I feel it in my bones."

"I hope you're right. I'm going to start right now."

"That's the spirit, M'sieu Nic. I know a little potion—"

"No potions!" he warned.

"You do not have to yell. I only want to help, to make her a little more willing to listen to reason."

"Please, Zareh. Don't help me anymore. This is something I must do on my own. Do you understand?"

"You know best, M'sieu Nic." Zareh's tone indicated no such belief.

When Jerralee returned home from work several of her relatives were assembled around Tante Olivette's kitchen table. They looked so grim that she thought something terrible must have happened.

"Are we having an emergency meeting?" she asked.

"Not quite, Cousin," Hercule said by way of explanation. "I've been appointed spokesman, so we can speed things along. This is just a little informal gathering to offer our support."

Jerralee frowned. "Support in what?"

"We want you to know that we don't believe a word of the nasty rumors bein' spread around the parish," he said.

"What rumors?"

Hercule heaved a mighty sigh and spoke to the floor. "Why, the ones about you and M'sieu Nic."

She shook her head. "What about us?"

"You must know that ever'body in Poulee Crossing has been talking about how he kissed you at the ball game," he pointed out.

"Oh, that." Jerralee laughed nervously. "He was just getting revenge for the hot dog incident. It didn't mean a thing."

"Well, that's not quite the full extent of it. We also hear tell that you and Nic Delarue..." his words trailed away meaningfully as he made a rolling gesture with his hand.

Ordinarily, Jerralee wouldn't have deigned to answer such accusations, but she did care what her family thought and spoke up in her own defense. "I've done nothing wrong."

Cousin Beatrix chimed in, "We're not saying whether it was wrong or right. Allasame, there are those who think you went to Baton Rouge with the man."

"I did go there." Jerralee had to raise her voice to be heard above the murmuring that had erupted at that statement. "But I went alone."

Hercule slumped in his chair. "I tell you true, I almost wish it were so. Then we could quit worrying about you allatime."

"Let me get this straight. Are you saying that you'd feel better if Nic and I *were* having an affair?" she asked incredulously.

"I'm just saying that the man would do right by you," Hercule hastened to explain.

Jerralee rolled her eyes. "Excuse me, have I stepped into a time warp or something? These are the nineties—the *nineteen* nineties. Men don't have 'to do right' by women anymore."

Hercule ignored her facetious remark. "M'sieu Nic has proven himself a good citizen. He is an honorable man."

"Make a damn fine husband, too," muttered another cousin.

At that moment someone pounded on the back door and Tante Olivette, who could see the caller from where she stood, clasped her hands over her heart dramatically.

"Poo-yie! It's a sign from above." She pushed open the screen door. "M'sieu Nic! Come in, come in."

"I just stopped by to see Jerralee," he said as he stepped through the door and looked around the room. "But if I'm interrupting something, I can come back another time."

"Actually you *are* interrupting something. Were you invited?" Jerralee glanced briefly at Nic, who looked wonderful in well-pressed gray slacks and a white turtleneck.

"Jerralee, that's no way for a young lady to greet a caller," Olivette admonished. "Where are your manners, *cher?*"

"Jerralee's right, I wasn't invited," Nic said gallantly. "I should have telephoned and made a proper date before barging in."

The assorted relatives were smiling and Jerralee wondered whose side they were on. "You and I are not dating," she pointed out.

"I was hoping to change that," he said with a smile. "That's what I wanted to talk to you about, but if you're busy. . ."

With a wide grin brightening his features, Hercule picked up his hat, a signal that his work was done. "Well, I don't suppose we need to worry about you anymore, Cousin. Especially not now that M'sieu Nic has come calling."

Only with the utmost control was Jerralee able to avoid stamping her foot. "He has not *come callin'*," she denied hotly. "And even if he has, you can't think that I'd be agreeable."

"Of course we can," Tante Olivette cried. "No man in the parish is more handsome or eligible."

"And you're not getting any younger, Minette," Nonc Albert reminded her.

Jerralee couldn't believe her family was discussing her marital status in front of Nic. "You're all impossible. You should be ashamed of yourselves."

Hercule stopped dead in his tracks, turned and faced the small group. "Does anyone in this family have a problem with M'sieu Nic sparking Minette?"

The unanimous vote proved that no one had any objection whatsoever. Obviously, Nic had already won them over. Assuming their matchmaking efforts had been successful the relatives soon dispersed to their suppers.

As they took their leave Jerralee's gaze got tangled up with Nic's, and she was hard-pressed to come up with a good reason to send him away. His eyes were so warm and caressing that she gamely followed him outside when Tante Olivette suggested they take a little walk along the bayou to finish their discussion.

The red sun was setting behind the cypress trees as they slipped out the back door and crossed the yard. Nonc Albert's hounds looked up lazily but did not stir. It was too close to feeding time to venture away from the house.

Jerralee fought the urge to touch Nic by plunging her hands into the back pockets of her jeans as they skirted the overgrown garden. A wide expanse of uncut grass sloped down to the bayou, and they walked side by side along a path beaten down by generations of LeBeaus in quest of crabs, catfish, shrimp and flounder.

"That was a dumb move on your part, Delarue." Jerralee was careful to keep her eyes on the path.

Nic walked beside her and longed to take her into his arms. "Before you say anything we'll both regret, will you do just one small thing for me?"

"I'm not going to let you kiss me again, if that's what you have in mind." She knew she had just admitted her vulnerability, but she didn't care. She'd done a lot of thinking while driving back to Poulee Crossing this morning, and she knew that spending time with Nic was dangerous. Liking Nic was dangerous, and loving him was the most dangerous thing of all. She had to maintain a distance because she feared she'd finally met her match.

In the wrong man.

He didn't speak, so she glanced up into his intense gaze. "Never again, Nic. Neither of us seems to be able to think or act rationally when we touch, and I don't like feeling out of control."

Nic was delighted by her unwitting confession. "I agree. You can relax, I'm not planning to kiss you. Not yet."

"Not ever," she insisted too passionately. "What *do* you want?"

"I want you to pretend that we've just met."

"That wouldn't change anything."

"Humor me."

Jerralee wasn't sure she wanted to go along with him on this, it was too simple. "If I play your little game, then will you go away?"

He held on to his optimism. "If that's what you want."

"Okay," she sighed. "We just met."

"Let's pretend that my name is Nic Smith, and you're—"

"Don't tell me, Jerralee Jones. It sounds like something on a billboard with the words Girls! Girls! Girls! in capital letters."

Nic grinned. "Do you like me, Ms. Jones?"

She shook her head, but before she could speak, he reminded, "And keep in mind that my name is Smith."

She began to see where this role-playing was leading and tried to think of something she disliked about him besides his family ties. She couldn't. "Yes."

"That's promising," he said softly. "Because I like you, too. Would you be willing to get to know me better? Maybe even go out with me?"

"You mean on a *date?*"

"It is the custom."

She planned to say no, but what came out was, "I don't know."

"Come on, *cher,* you've dated every other guy in the parish. What's wrong with me?" Nic was surprised at the jealousy that gnawed at him.

"I'm just trying to be honest and that's hard to do when we're playing a game." Jerralee bent down to pick up a pretty stone, which gave her something to do with her hands.

"Call me Mr. Smith. Maybe it'll help." Nic draped an arm around her shoulders, but she ducked away.

"All right, Mr. Smith, I think I would enjoy going out with you."

"You've made me a happy man, Ms. Jones."

"But I think it's only fair to warn you that my family is planning to marry me off to the first eligible man who comes along."

"I'll take my chances."

"I'm not sure I'm willing to take mine."

"Neither was I in the beginning." He smiled at her tenderly. "But I think I must have fallen in love with you."

"What?"

"I guess it started the night we spent in the attic, *cher.* I was hopelessly charmed."

"I was terrible that night," she recalled.

"Yes, you were. Terribly beautiful."

She covered her ears. "I won't listen to this."

Nic took her hands in his. "I want us to be completely honest with each other and that's why I had to tell you."

"I don't want you to love me," she cried. She really didn't, because knowing he loved her just made it more difficult to repress her own feelings.

"I know. I didn't want it to happen, either. God knows, I fought it. But as they say in old movies, this thing is bigger than the both of us."

She was running out of artillery in the face of his conviction. "You don't think I'm good enough for you."

"That's ridiculous."

"Then why didn't you want to love me? And remember," she said, borrowing his own phrase. "We're being totally honest here."

"You've always rejected my overtures, and you've given me nothing but trouble. I guess I didn't know how to love you."

"And now you do?"

"I haven't a clue," he confessed brightly. "I just knew I had to get this out in the open."

"I wouldn't dream of betraying my family by falling in love with one of their enemies."

He grasped her shoulders. "I am *not* the enemy, Jerralee. When will you get that through that thick little skull of yours? When you can't handle the situation, you fall back on that senseless feud. You use it like a shield to keep me from getting too close to you."

She turned her face away from him. As dusk gathered, a choir of frogs commenced their nocturne. Insects chirped in the grass, and water hyacinths floated lazily on the bayou. The moss-draped cypresses and live oaks cast mystical shadows around them, and borne on a soft breeze came the tantalizing aroma of bubbling gumbo.

"What do you expect me to do, Nic? Melt into a little puddle just because the rich man who lives in the mansion says he loves me?"

Nic sighed his exasperation. "You're behaving exactly as I expected. You're lashing out at me because you're afraid of your own feelings."

"I am not," she lied.

"Think about it, Jerralee. A moment ago you were angry because I told you I had fought against loving you. Now you're fighting because I do love you."

She refused to admit he was right, so she said nothing at all.

Nic recognized her silence for what it was, and because he loved her so much he allowed her to get away with it, this time. "I care about you in spite of our differences, maybe even because of them. All I know is they're really insignificant."

"Insignificant?" she sputtered as she thought about all the things keeping them apart.

"They're insignificant because I love you."

Her heart leaped at his words. She had secretly hoped to actually hear them, and now she realized how afraid they made her feel. "It would never work."

"I'm not asking you to marry me," he said gently. When he noticed a shadow of regret cloud her bright eyes, he added, "Not yet, *cher*. We have a lot to sort through before we reach that point."

Inexplicably disappointed, she asked, "What exactly are you asking me to do?"

"I want us to spend some time together. And if, after a while, you decide to end our relationship because you can't love me back, then so be it. I just want you to be honest with yourself and with me."

"This honesty business is not so easy," she replied with all the aplomb she could muster.

"I know." He smiled in the growing darkness. "But are you willing to try?"

"I'm afraid to try."

He gathered her into his arms and clasped his hand behind her waist. He smiled down into her eyes. "But are you willing to try, *cher?*"

She felt as though she were navigating the swamp in a leaky pirogue. But wrapped in Nic's warm embrace all things seemed possible.

"I'll try," she whispered.

Chapter Nine

Nic called Jerralee the very next morning and told her of his decision. Her silence confused him. "I thought you'd be pleased to hear the news." He had hoped her excitement would keep her from asking too many questions.

She should have been thrilled by this new turn of events, but she wasn't, and she didn't know why. "I'm just surprised, that's all."

Nic knew he was taking a risk, but the ends justified the means. "I'm sending you a check by private messenger. It should be there before long."

"You were able to find a good handwriting sample to authenticate the IOU?" she asked skeptically.

"Do you honestly think I'd pay this debt if I didn't believe you were entitled to the money?" The evasion was a necessary one. For over a hundred years the Delarues had profited from land they'd acquired from the LeBeaus under questionable circumstances. Now that he'd come to know them, he knew Jerralee's family deserved something for all they'd lost. Eighteen thousand dollars wasn't nearly enough, but it was a beginning.

"I suppose not."

"Will you start work on Sweetwood right away?" he asked.

Jerralee's suspicion gave way to excitement as she discussed her plans for renovating the plantation house. What was her problem anyway, this was what she had wanted, wasn't it?

"I'll call a family meeting tonight."

"Tonight?" He gave voice to his disappointment. "I had hoped we could celebrate this evening."

Jerralee laughed. "What would you be celebrating?"

"Many things," he said mysteriously. "Our first real date for one."

"Nic, I've been thinking about that."

"Now, *cher,* we talked this all out last night. We agreed to give ourselves a chance."

When he called her *cher* in that tone of voice she found it impossible to use good judgment. "We can get together after the meeting."

"That's good for me. I'll pick you up at eight."

"I'll be ready."

"Oh, and dress casually," he said mysteriously. "We'll have formal evenings together, but this won't be one of them."

At the meeting, none of the LeBeaus had questioned Nic's motives in paying the old debt. When

Jerralee expressed her misgivings, they pooh-poohed her into silence. There was something fishy about a Delarue giving in to a LeBeau without a bigger fight, but when Nic arrived she forgot all about such things.

He was prompt and, as promised, casually dressed in jeans and a blue knit shirt. He chatted amiably as he drove, but wouldn't reveal their destination despite Jerralee's many questions.

"Don't you know what curiosity did to the cat, *cher?*" he teased.

She got her first clue as to where they were going when they arrived at a local marina—apparently their date involved a boat ride. It was nearly dark when Nic helped her into a shiny custom-fitted airboat, and they took off across the bayou at a fast clip. The boat's lights flashed through the water, and the warm, humid air was heavy with the smell of the bayou. The wind rifled Nic's hair, and Jerralee secured her own wind-whipped locks with a knotted bandana.

After several minutes she relaxed against the plush leather seat. She looked over at Nic and realized all over again how devastatingly handsome he was. How was it possible that this man loved her? Did she have the courage to entrust her heart to a man she had never thought to trust at all? Nic Delarue was nothing like she had expected he'd be.

She had thought he would be selfish, but he was kind and generous. Instead of being arrogant, he seemed hardly aware of his good looks and wealth. She had assumed he was aloof because he considered himself above others, but now she knew better. Nic had been lonely. And, from what she had learned, he had always been lonely.

Because his father had told him he was different from his neighbors, beautiful Nic had worried that he would not be accepted.

She'd thought him cruel, but she was the cruel one for having assumed the worst of a man she had not allowed herself to know. Perhaps she had been the arrogant one, as well.

Jerralee was getting used to this new self-analysis, but it made her uncomfortable just the same. She called out above the roar of the powerful engine, "Where are we going, Nic?"

He maneuvered the boat expertly around an exposed cypress knee, then turned to her and smiled. "To a place I like to go when the stars are out like they are tonight."

It was fully dark now, and the sky was a purple canopy filled with glittering, far-flung stars. A bright slice of moon hung over the treetops.

Nic slowed the boat as he steered it more deeply into the swamp. Like sentinels, moss-draped cypress trees guarded their realm, the lacy strands dripping almost to the water.

"The Indians called Spanish moss tree hair," he told her. "Legend says they're the long locks, turned silver-gray, of an Indian maiden and her beloved, who died for love under an oak. Their hair was cut by a great spirit and draped on a tree, spreading through the years to other trees as a testimony to eternal love."

"I've heard that story before. But I think it's a little farfetched," she admitted. "Pretty, but farfetched."

"Don't you believe in eternal love?" he teased.

"I don't know," she said honestly.

"Henry Wadsworth likened the moss waving on the cypresses to 'banners that hang on the walls of ancient cathedrals,'" he quoted.

"That image is a little easier to accept." She looked at him uneasily. "I guess you should know— I'm not very romantic."

"No problem, I'm romantic enough for the both of us."

After a few more minutes Jerralee spotted a tiny island in the middle of the swamp. It was a green mound, rising out of the dark waters like the back of a giant turtle. As they drew closer the boat's lights revealed that the knoll was covered with a thick carpet of wildflowers. A mockingbird welcomed them from an orange tree.

Nic guided the boat through the ever-present water hyacinths, fragile green and lavender flowers that were called orchids of the bayous by some. Others, especially those who made their living on the waterways, considered the plant a menace. An ever-invading, advancing army of fragile subversives that filled the waterways with a floating garden of tightly packed waxlike leaves. Colorless strings of roots extended several feet below the surface and made navigation difficult in some places.

The plant was not native to Louisiana, but to Japan. It had gotten its tenacious hold when samples were given to visitors at the International Cotton Exposition of 1884 in New Orleans. People had taken them home and placed them in ponds and waterways, where the plants had found a lush affinity in the warm, shallow waters of the Louisiana lowlands.

"Here we are." Nic guided the boat to the edge of the island.

"This is our destination?" she asked as he took her hand and helped her out of the boat and onto firmer footing.

"It's a special place." Nic turned back to the boat and retrieved a large picnic hamper and a thick quilt from the storage compartment. "If you'll carry the quilt, I'll get the lantern."

He lit the lamp, which cast a soft yellow glow around them like the light of a dozen candles. Taking her hand, he guided her up the slope.

Jerralee frowned. "It's awfully lonely here, isn't it?"

"Are you afraid I'll do something dastardly?" When she hesitated too long before answering, he said, "I won't hurt you, *cher*. Don't you know that?"

"I know." That wasn't her main concern. She was more afraid of her own reaction than of any action Nic might take. "Lead on."

When they reached the top of the knoll Nic took the quilt and spread it over a bed of fragrant flowers. "Have you had your supper yet, *cher?*"

"Tante Olivette puts supper on the table every night promptly at six." She didn't admit that she'd been too nervous to do more than take three or four bites, a fact that hadn't gone unnoticed by her aunt and uncle.

"Maybe later than," he said as he set the basket to one side. Nic lounged in the middle of the quilt and patted the empty spot beside him before clasping his hands behind his head. "Sit down, I promise not to bite."

Jerralee sat stiffly away from him, waiting for his next move. "Why did you bring me here, Nic?"

"Relax, *cher.*"

"I can't."

"Sure you can. All we're going to do is talk and look at the stars. I promise."

"I have your word on that?"

"You do. I won't touch you or kiss you unless you ask me to do so."

That was what she was afraid of. Jerralee sighed and lay down beside him, careful to keep some distance between them. "I don't know much about the stars. Tell me about them."

"Neither do I, but I know beauty when I see it."

She rolled her head in his direction and found him looking directly at her. She quickly turned her gaze back to the heavens.

"Look, is that Cassiopeia?" she asked, pointing to a six-starred constellation.

"Yes. I'm not sure exactly how the myth goes, but wasn't she the wife of King Cepheus? The one who was changed into a constellation because she went around boasting how pretty she was?"

"Could be," she allowed. "I never was into that stuff."

"I don't believe it," Nic teased. "A good old-fashioned, superstitious girl like you not interested in heavenly bodies?"

"I'm not so superstitious," she denied. "Tell me some more stories."

"I'd like nothing better than to impress you with my knowledge of astronomy, but none comes to mind. I'll study up on it someday and dazzle your socks off."

Jerralee chuckled. "I'll be looking forward to it." It wouldn't be wise to let him know that she was already dazzled. "I like your special place. Do you come here often?"

"Sometimes. I'm glad you like it."

"I assumed you preferred the faster pace of life found in New Orleans or Baton Rouge."

"I enjoy an occasional party, but I don't care for it as a steady diet."

Jerralee could feel his gaze upon her, and knew that if she looked at him she would be in danger of being kissed. She turned her head.

The expected kiss wasn't forthcoming. He didn't reach out for her but kept his hands locked behind his head and whispered, "My lips ache with the need to touch yours."

Jerralee had never known such raw and primitive desire as she did at that moment. "What are you going to do about it?"

"Nothing."

"Nothing?"

"I promised, *cher*. And I try never to break promises."

"I see."

"However, there's nothing to keep *you* from kissing *me*, if you feel so inclined."

Jerralee wondered if it was the quarter moon that had affected her so strangely, because the next moment she raised up on one elbow and traced the outline of his lips with her finger. "I feel so inclined."

Her kiss was as light as a firefly's caress, as gentle as the summer breeze wafting softly across the water. But the flames it ignited were anything but soothing.

Nic clenched his hands tightly to keep from reaching for her and crushing her body to his. His promise kept his passion in check.

Jerralee trailed her fingers down the strong column of his neck in a silken caress and flattened her chest against his. He felt her heart beating double cadence and he groaned with the need to put his arms around her. Why had he made such an impossible pact?

She responded mindlessly to the magic of his lips, and though he made no move to touch her with any other part of his body, his lips sought a deeper commitment. She opened her mouth a bit and his tongue played havoc with her senses. He nibbled on her bottom lip and melting pleasure reminded her that she should stop this wonderful madness. Reluctantly she pulled away.

"Do your lips still ache?" she asked in a voice so husky she barely recognized it as her own.

"More than ever," he replied. "But most of the pain has moved south."

Jerralee laughed. "You're outrageous, Nicolas Delarue."

"I'm also hungry. Let's see what Zareh put in that basket." He sat up and began unloading the contents on the quilt. Zareh had prepared a bacchanalian feast: cold shrimp with a spicy dipping sauce, deviled eggs, a piquant rice salad, cheesecake and fruit.

Everything was served on pretty china plates, with silver utensils. The mint-green napkins coordinated with the floral china pattern. There was even a long-stemmed white rose in a bud vase and two candlesticks for the middle of the "table."

Jerralee couldn't believe it. "I've never been to a white-tie picnic before, only the bologna sandwich and potato chip variety. Maybe I should have dressed a little more formally." She looked in distaste at her jeans, purple cotton top and sneakers.

"You look lovely. You could wear a sugar sack and I'd still see you in silk."

"You really are a romantic, aren't you?" There was wonderment in her voice.

He only smiled as he poured sauvignon blanc into thin crystal wineglasses and made a toast. "To a wonderful beginning. May it never end."

They tapped their glasses together and sipped wine that had somehow been chilled to the perfect temperature. A chorus of insects and frogs provided background music as they ate. They talked and discovered more about each other, learning all the things that made falling in love so much fun.

After they finished the food and repacked the hamper Nic pulled out a battery-powered cassette recorder and switched it on. At first the sound of Righteous Brothers ballads seemed alien on the sultry night air, but soon it became as natural as the other night sounds. Nic pulled Jerralee to her feet.

"Dancing doesn't count as touching," he whispered in her ear as he waltzed her around.

"It sure feels like touching," she murmured.

"Just relax."

"I can't believe this."

"What?"

"That I just had a candlelit supper in the middle of the swamp and now I'm dancing to the Righteous Brothers under the stars."

"You mean you've never done that before?" he asked with exaggerated surprise.

"No! Have you?"

"All the time."

When he laughed she punched his arm. "You haven't really, have you?"

"No," he told her. "I didn't even think of it until I met you."

How was it that he always knew what to say? "Will you kiss me?"

"Is that an official request?"

In answer, she cupped his face in her hands and pulled his lips down to hers. Their kiss ignited and they slipped down to the quilt, entangled in a languid embrace. The Righteous Brothers sang about losin' that lovin' feeling, but Nic and Jerralee didn't have that problem. They wrapped their arms around each other and pressed their bodies close, kissing and touching and discovering each other in ways that spoke louder than words.

The scent of wild jasmine drifted over the lovers, and the night sky was ablaze with rhinestone stars. Breathless, they fell apart and stared up at the heavens. At that moment a shooting star burned its way across the sky and to Jerralee it seemed an omen.

"I wonder if that means our relationship will be hot but short-lived?" She joked to break the tension that had grown between them.

"Maybe it means it will last a lifetime," Nic said softly. "That meteor is part of a universe that was formed millions of years ago."

"Do you always have the right answers?"

"No. Sometimes I don't even know the right questions."

"Tonight has been lovely, Nic, but I think we should go."

He leaned over, kissed her again and then jumped to his feet. "As you wish, my lady." He pulled her up, folded the quilt and picked up the empty hamper. She carried the lantern to light their way, and arm in arm, they walked back to the boat and the real world.

When they got to her home Nic walked her up to the front door. "Would you think badly of me if I asked to be released from that rash promise I made earlier?"

Feeling bold and warm after such an unbelievably romantic evening, Jerralee didn't hesitate. "Consider yourself released."

The words were barely out of her mouth before he pulled her hips into his own and their thighs touched. He wrapped his arms around her and slanted his lips over hers. She silently voted him undisputed master of slow, burning kisses and her lips parted in welcome. A soft sigh escaped when their tongues met.

"Nic," she cautioned a moment later, "what if someone sees us?"

"Too dark," he mumbled. He lowered his head and watched as her eyelids fluttered shut and her lips trembled in anticipation. Gently, he kissed her temple, then the curve of her eyebrow, the tip of her nose. When his thumb brushed her bottom lip, she pressed herself closer. Jerralee sighed again. If this was the real world, her fantasy life would never be the same.

* * *

During the next few weeks Jerralee spent all her free time working on a formal business plan for the craft guild. She recruited various relatives to help with the renovations on Sweetwood, while she, Tante Olivette and Cousin Beatrix hired artisans and screened various crafts made by local residents. Together they also developed a complete inventory line for the guild.

Her tenacity and enthusiasm, along with her well-documented business plan, enabled her to get a loan from a bank in Baton Rouge. Sweetwood Craft Guild was on its way to becoming a reality.

Nic was impressed with her hard work and entrepreneurial spirit and offered to donate a few acres around Sweetwood for conversion to parking areas and gardens. Jerralee wouldn't accept such a gift, but agreed to the proposition on the condition that he be paid for the land out of the first year's profits. A deal was quickly struck and shook on.

Nic was always available to offer advice, insight and a helping hand. For the first time in her life Jerralee found herself caught up in the joy of becoming part of a couple. Many evenings they worked side by side at the plantation house. Sometimes Nic took her to the movies or out to eat at a favorite seafood shanty, but when he told her he wanted her to come to his place for dinner, she balked.

He tried again one night while they were sitting in the swing on the gallery. Nic wrapped his arm around her shoulders. "Won't you come? I've invited Marcus and Jeanne."

She relaxed against his broad chest. "I don't think so."

His lips brushed her temple as he said, "They're the only close friends I have, and I want you to meet them."

"What if they disapprove of me?"

He took her left hand in his and absently caressed her fingers. "How can they, when you're so perfect?"

"But what if they do?"

He nuzzled her ear. "Then I'd give them up. It wouldn't be that much of a hardship. Since they had the baby, they've become quite boring." He snuggled her in his arms.

She nudged him in the ribs with her elbow. "Be serious."

"I am. I'm seriously in love with you."

Jerralee read the truth in his eyes. "Okay, I'll come to your dinner party."

Nic's smile was tender. "Shall we seal it with a kiss?"

The St. Pierres proved to be an attractive, warm-hearted couple and Jerralee was glad Nic had talked her into coming. After dinner they settled in the living room for coffee and a lively discussion of the mischief the two men had engaged in when they were boys.

"Speaking of children," Marcus said as he reached into his pocket and pulled out a handful of pictures.

Nic winked at Jerralee.

"Were we discussing children, Jerralee?" Jeanne asked. She put her hand over her husband's and shook her head. "No, darling, I think not."

Nic moved from his position by the mantel and sat down on the sofa beside Jerralee. "It appears we have reached that point in the evening when Marcus begins to experience withdrawal symptoms."

Everyone laughed but Marcus.

"I thought you might be interested in your godson's latest snapshots, but I can see you're not."

Being a godparent in Louisiana was not something to be taken lightly. If the parents died or couldn't provide for their child the godfather took over, and was happy to do it.

Jerralee had never thought of Nic taking on such a heavy burden and she was curious. "I would like to see the pictures, Marcus."

Nic and Jeanne groaned.

Marcus smiled smugly and brought the pictures to her. He sat down beside her to explain each one. "Little fellow isn't even two years old, yet he speaks quite plainly. He's reaching for the camera in this one. Isn't that cute?"

"It's adorable," she agreed. "What's his name?"

"Paul Nicolas, after Jeanne's father and old Nic here. In this one he was upset because I wouldn't let him have the camera."

Nic put his arm around Jerralee and looked over her shoulder. "That's amazing."

Marcus beamed. "He is something."

"No," Nic teased. "I think it's amazing that there is something that you wouldn't give him."

Jeanne giggled. "Paul did get it in the end."

"You're spoiling the finale," Marcus said. "Jeanne snapped this one with her camera." It was a picture of

Marcus trying to rescue his expensive camera before little Paul could bang it on the floor.

After the pictures had all been shown and remarked on, Marcus put them away.

"Is that all you brought with you, Marc?" Nic teased.

"That's all," his friend said with a bright grin as he crossed to Jeanne's chair. He put his hands on her shoulders and she smiled up at him, nodding. "Next time I'll bring the videos."

Everyone groaned. Nic absently caressed Jerralee's shoulder. "It's a good thing they only have one child or we might have to look at pictures all night."

"We're changing that in about six months," Marc announced with a smile.

Jerralee wondered if she was the only one who noticed the flash of regret clouding Nic's eyes before he jumped to his feet to congratulate his best friend.

Nic was truly happy for his friends, and thoroughly ashamed of the momentary stab of envy he'd felt upon hearing their good news.

"If you want the job, we'd like you to be godfather again, Nic," Jeanne said. "The ultrasound tells us this one will be a girl."

The party broke up soon afterward. Marc insisted Jeanne needed her rest and after the couple left, Jerralee prepared to go.

"Don't go," Nic coaxed as he put his hands on her waist. "Can't you stay a little longer?"

She slid her hands up the lapels of his jacket to rest on his shoulders. "Maybe a little longer."

"I've been aching to do this for hours," he said as he pulled her body against his. "I want to kiss you so badly."

"I'd rather you kissed me well," she teased. A tantalizing thrill of anticipation coursed through her as she raised her lips to meet his. It was at moments like this that she was tempted to voice her love for him, and yet she clung stubbornly to her reserve.

Caution was soon overcome by need and Jerralee's sigh of pleasure prompted Nic to deepen the kiss. His sweet touch wrapped her in a quivery nimbus of desire.

Nic nuzzled her neck. "Hold me, Jerralee," he said in a breathy whisper. "I need you to hold me." He needed more than that. He suspected that she was falling in love with him and he needed to hear her say the words.

She held him, longing to tell him how much she cared, but afraid to speak. There were still too many obstacles between them, some of which might prove impossible to overcome.

"I'd better go," she whispered, incapable of normal speech. But she made no move to leave the warm haven of his arms.

Nic leaned back against the door and the hands that lazily gripped her waist belied his anxiety. "Do you really want to leave?"

She shook her head. "Not really."

"How do you feel about me right now?"

"That's not a fair question."

"I know. Answer it anyway."

"I care about you, Nic. You must know that."

"I know that."

"Then why did you ask?"

"I just wanted to hear you say so. Would you say it again?"

"I care about you. Very much."

"I love you, Jerralee LeBeau, and I think you love me, too."

"You're awfully sure of yourself, aren't you?" she teased in an effort to lighten the mood.

"Sure enough to ask you to marry me."

Afraid that Nic might see what was in her heart by looking into her eyes, she wrenched herself away and turned her back to him. "Now I know I should be going."

He reached out and took her hand in his. "Don't run away from me, *cher*." He turned her around and caressed her jaw with his free hand. "If you don't love me, say so. But don't run from me."

"Nic, why do you have to make it so difficult?"

"That isn't my intention. Don't you love me? Not even a little bit?"

"Of course I do, but—"

Nic pulled her into his arms and she glimpsed the raw emotion that pooled in his eyes before his lips found hers. Her heart shattered in the hot hunger of his kiss. His tongue sent shivers of desire threading through her as it traced the soft fullness of her lips and explored the recesses of her mouth.

His lips left hers only to taste her earlobe, then made their way down the side of her neck. "Do you want to marry me, *cher?*"

"Yes, but—"

He silenced her protest with a hard, quick kiss. "Just yes will do."

"Nic—" Jerralee didn't finish because he kissed away her words. She'd been about to say that nothing had really changed. But he made her forget all about reason and logic and the obstacles that stood between them.

the world. Now I have come to my own country to show allegiance... and that I do not forget all about... Lockerby woman...

Chapter Ten

Jerralee didn't remember moving into the living room. She only became aware of where they were when Nic stopped kissing her long enough to settle her onto his lap. He drew her back into the warm circle of his arms and held her close to his urgent body. Her arms found their way around his neck and she clung to him, letting his vitality seep into her senses. Despite his passion, there was gentleness in the way his mouth slanted over hers.

When her tongue parted his lips searchingly, Nic was shaken by the intensity of his desire. He cupped the soft swell of her breast, and gently outlined the circle of flesh that surged against his hand. He couldn't suppress a triumphant groan when he heard her murmur of surrender.

From the doorway came the familiar jingle of Zareh's silver bracelets. Hearing the sound, Nic reluctantly withdrew his hand and smiled at Jerralee's frustrated protest. Cupping her face in both his hands, he bestowed a quick parting kiss on her lips.

Nic's voice was strained when he spoke. "I hope you have a good reason for this interruption, Zareh."

For Jerralee that was the first inkling she had that anyone else was still in the house. Or in the universe for that matter. Embarrassed, she snuggled against Nic.

Zareh did not seem the least bit flustered at finding them in a somewhat compromising position.

"I try to tell that silly man it was his own job to take care of problems at the mill, that he shouldn't be bothering M'sieu Nic when he is busy. But he jus' keep on demanding that you come to the mill right away. He says somet'ing is broken, I don't remember what." Zareh shrugged. "You want me to call him back and tell him—"

"No, I'll take care of it," Nic interrupted.

The tall woman left the room grumbling about men and machines and bad timing.

Jerralee and Nic stood, but when she would have moved away from him, he pulled her into his arms. He looked into her eyes and said, "I asked you to marry me, *cher*. Do I get an answer now or will you torture me a little longer?"

"Give me time, Nic."

He was afraid that if she thought too long, she might dream up yet another reason why it wouldn't work. "Very well, you have ten or twenty minutes. Use them wisely."

She smiled. "How generous of you."

He kissed the tip of her nose. "Will you wait for me?"

"If you promise to hurry back."

He laughed. "That's one promise I don't have to worry about breaking."

After he left Jerralee waited impatiently in the living room. Doubts surfaced, but she managed to squelch each one in turn. She truly loved Nic and she felt his love for her. During the past weeks he had carefully planted the seeds of trust in her heart. He'd nurtured them with honesty and tenderness until the love between them had bloomed like an everlasting rose.

What harm was there in ending a stupid feud that had long since lost its meaning? Nic had willingly donated his time to help get the craft guild started and had proven generous beyond measure. The rest of the family had practically adopted him and took it for granted that she and Nic would marry. Uniting the LeBeaus and Delarues in marriage was the logical way to finally lay the old hostilities to rest.

The important thing, she told herself as she relaxed and stretched on the comfortable sofa, was their love. What could be more perfect than that?

After a few minutes Zareh came into the room. "I brought you a *tasse,* Mam'selle. It will help pass the time until M'sieu Nic comes home."

"Thank you, Zareh." The woman missed very little that went on in the house, Jerralee thought as she accepted the cup of rich, black coffee.

"He is a fine man, *non?*"

"Yes, he is."

"And you are a fine, strong woman. The marriage will be good and you will make many fine *bébés*."

"Well," Jerralee hedged. "Nic and I haven't resolved the issue of marriage yet."

"It will come, this I know. I tell M'sieu a long time ago that you will come to him and did you not?"

"Yes," Jerralee said softly, her superstitious nature making her suddenly suspicious. "You did."

"See," she said smugly. "Ol' Zareh, she knows these t'ings." She floated down onto the opposite end of the sofa, arranging her colorful burnoose artistically around her. "Now, we shall plan the wedding."

"That might be a bit premature."

"*Non*, these t'ings take time. We must begin now." Zareh appeared to consider the possibilities. "It will be a grand worthy affair." Her eyes lit up with sudden inspiration. "Perhaps we can duplicate the Durand sisters' double wedding! But with only one bride and groom, of course."

"The Durand sisters?"

Zareh frowned. "Have you not heard of the wealthy Durands? They were a planter family who lived on Teche Bayou back before the trouble between the states. M'sieu Durand was very rich and believed that riches should be enjoyed. He found the most incredible ways to spend money, that man."

"What about the wedding?"

"Oh, that. When his two daughters announced their engagements he wanted a wedding like no other. He ordered a cargo of big spiders from Cathay. Some people say they came only from the woods near Catahoula, but I like to think of them as great China spiders. It makes a better tale.

"Allasame, they were very large and capable of large deeds. Days before the wedding them spiders were set loose in the long avenue of live oaks that led up to the *maison*. The slaves watched the spiders working, lacing the spaces between the trees with yards and yards of delicate webs.

"Ever'body worry that it might rain before the wedding and wash away all that work, but M'sieu Durand never worry."

"Did it rain?" Jerralee asked.

"Of course not. M'sieu Durand was a charmed man that way. He call' out his slaves and give them bellows and bags of silver and gold dust. Over the long canopies they worked, spreading the fairy dust. Others worked beneath, laying down carpets to cover the three-mile passage under the trees. At one end they set up an open-air altar, and all along the sides were tables laden with all kinds of delicious food. It was a beautiful wedding, right out of a fairy tale." Zareh wiped an errant tear of nostalgia from her eye.

Jerralee smiled doubtfully. "Is the story true?"

"Oh yes, my *m'mère* tell me and her *m'mère* told it to her."

"It certainly sounds grand."

"A bit too grand for Poulee Crossing, perhaps," the older woman said dismissively. "We must come up with another idea."

Jerralee was glad the notion of giant spiders had been abandoned and tried to steer Zareh off the subject of weddings altogether. "Tell me about Nic's childhood."

"Later. Now we must plan the wedding," she insisted. "It is my responsibility. If not for me, mebbe there not be a wedding at all. I got you and M'sieu together, and now the curse will be lifted and there will be plenty Delarue heirs."

"Even if Nic and I were married tomorrow, we couldn't have a child before his thirty-fifth birthday." Jerralee had almost forgotten about the curse and it made her sad to think that they might be childless if they married.

"Allasame it will be done."

"I suppose we could adopt children," Jerralee said thoughtfully.

"No need. M'sieu Nic will give you many fine *bébés*. It was I," Zareh exclaimed proudly, "who learned that the only way to lift the curse was for him to marry a LeBeau."

Jerralee's rosy reverie was replaced by shock. "What?"

"You marry M'sieu and the curse will be gone. Poof!" she pronounced happily.

"Does Nic know about that?"

"*Oui*. I tell him myself. That is why I must help plan the wedding. It is I who made it happen, and it will be I who make it glorious."

Jerralee was still trying to take it all in. So Nic had to marry a LeBeau to end the curse? That explained so many things. "I don't believe this," she muttered with a sinking heart.

"Neither did M'sieu Nic," Zareh said with a smug smile. "At first."

Now Jerralee understood why Nic had swept her off her feet with romantic dates. Why he had pushed her to accept his proposal. There were no other eligible LeBeau women of marrying age. That's why he had claimed to love her. When he'd kissed her he'd been thinking of the curse and the fact that time was running out for him to win a LeBeau bride.

No, she argued with herself. It couldn't be true. Nic didn't believe in the curse. He'd told her so many times. But perhaps he had protested so vehemently in order to conceal his true feelings. Yet, it wasn't possible. He wouldn't marry a woman unless he truly loved her, would he?

But did he love her? Or had Zareh put a lovespell on him? On both of them? Now that she thought about it, everything about their meeting and subsequent courtship had been strange. There was the night they'd been locked in an unlocked attic. And the night she'd spent in Baton Rouge because of an unlikely coincidence. And what about the way her good sense seemed to desert her whenever he was around?

With Nic she felt an attraction more powerful than any she'd ever felt before, and she had often wondered what made it so strong. The last few weeks had seemed too good to be true, and maybe they were. Maybe they were the result of black magic.

Jerralee's voice was a hoarse whisper when she finally found it. "I have to go home."

"But you promised to wait for M'sieu Nic," Zareh protested.

"I can't stay." She grabbed her purse and beat a hasty retreat before the tears started. She made it all the way home and to the safety of her room before the flood began.

She didn't know what was true anymore. But now that the doubt had been raised, she couldn't believe unequivocally in Nic's love. Not when it was possible that he only wanted her to further the Delarue line. And not when both of them might have been unwitting victims of Zareh's voodoo charms.

The next two days were a nightmare of indecision for Jerralee. She didn't work and confined herself to her room. With no explanation for her behavior, she instructed her family to refuse Nic's hourly phone calls on her behalf. When he stopped by the house she told them to send him away.

Tante Olivette complied at first, giving her niece the benefit of the doubt. But by the second day she was determined to find out what had made Jerralee so unhappy.

"Minette," she cajoled. "Why you don't put that boy out of his misery and marry him?" She made herself comfortable in the only chair in Jerralee's room.

Jerralee brushed her hair ruthlessly. She avoided her aunt's direct gaze, but she could see her reflection in the dressing table mirror. "He is not in misery, *Tante.*"

"You won't see him, so how can you know?"

Jerralee stood up and paced the floor. "If I wanted to see him, I would. Okay?"

"Then maybe you would like to see someone else. Perhaps I could arrange something."

"I don't want any more of your blind dates. Ever!"

"If you won't see Nic, I can't change your hard head. But you must start keeping company with someone or you'll never get married."

"Then I'll be an old maid. A happy old maid." Jerralee flung open her closet, grabbed an old knapsack and began stuffing clothes into it. Fighting strong magic and her feelings for Nic were hard enough. She didn't have to stay around here and put up with her family's meddling.

"Where are you going, Minette?" Tante Olivette wanted to know.

"Fishing," was all she would say. If ever there was a time to retreat to her father's old shack, this was it. Maybe in the silence and isolation of the swamp, she could come to grips with the problems she had to face.

She completed her packing and started for the door. Her aunt's voice called after her. "You can run away from many things, Minette, but you can't run away from love."

Nic's patience finally gave out when he discovered Jerralee was gone. Knowing her as well as he did, he had expected her to put off giving him an answer for a while. But he had not expected her to avoid him completely. He'd tried to understand her irrational behavior, but could not. Obviously, her refusal to speak to him meant that she had rejected his proposal.

He wasn't sure what her unexplained disappearance meant, but he knew it was no way to treat someone you loved. She did love him, she had said so. Something had made her change her mind. Why had she taken the coward's way out? Jerralee was much too brave for that.

The more he thought about it, the more determined Nic became. If she didn't want to spend the rest of her life with him, she would have to tell him so to his face. Whatever puny objections she might still make couldn't stand up to true love. He would change her mind. But first he would have to find her.

He questioned all her family members but to no avail. He finally ended up on Tante Olivette's porch, sipping iced coffee.

"You don't seem very worried about Jerralee's disappearance," he said.

"She'll be back," the older woman said sagely. "What did you do to my girl to upset her so?"

"I asked her to marry me."

Olivette's eyes brightened. "And what was her answer?"

"She didn't give me one. A problem came up at the mill and I had to go and take care of it. She promised to wait for me, but when I came back she was gone."

"She had too much time to think. You should have married her quick."

"That was my intention until she ran away. I don't know where she is. I've asked around and no one will tell me anything. Do you have any ideas?"

"I know," she said calmly. "But Jerralee would never speak to me again if I told you."

Nic frowned and sat back in his chair. "You would stand in the way of true love?"

Olivette looked aghast. "No one wants her to marry you more than I do."

"And you still won't tell me where she is?"

"She made me swear not to." The older woman's pain was significant.

"I see."

"If you are worthy of her love, you won't give up so easily." She shook her head. "You could figure it out if you tried."

"I have tried."

Olivette sighed at his obtuseness. "She takes after her father, you know?"

"Does she?" he asked absently.

"Oh my, yes." She peered at Nic expectantly. "Tiboy used to go fishing when he was upset."

That comment brought back memories of the night he and Jerralee had spent in the attic. He'd worried then that her family would think she had come to harm if she stayed out all night. What had she said? He tried to recall.

Oh yes, Jerralee had explained that they would think she'd retreated to her father's old fishing shack in the swamp.

"She went fishing?" he asked incredulously.

"I never said—"

Nic kissed her wrinkled cheek and stopped her in midsentence. "Thank you, Tante Olivette."

"Allasame, you didn't hear it from me!"

"No, of course not," he said as he jumped up to leave.

"If you do happen to find Jerralee, you remind her of the engagement celebration tomorrow night for Cousin Deidre. And you can come, too."

Nic bounded down the front steps. At the bottom he stopped and grinned. "Keep the accordions warmed up and the gumbo hot. You're going to have another engagement to celebrate soon!"

Nic hurried home to Long Shadows to change into jeans and boots. He was on his way downstairs when he realized he hadn't the faintest notion of how to find

Tiboy LeBeau's fishing shack. While he was pondering that, Zareh joined him in the foyer.

"Are you going out, M'sieu Nic?"

"I know where Jerralee is and—"

Zareh clasped her hands and smiled. "That is good. Now you will go to her and straighten everyt'ing out."

"If that is possible."

"She will understand," Zareh said with some certainty. "The night you went to the mill we had a long talk and I fear she got some wrong ideas."

Nic looked at Zareh sharply. "What kind of wrong ideas?"

She began to recount their conversation, but Nic interrupted. "I've already heard the spider story, just skip to what you said after that."

"Very well."

By the time Zareh was finished Nic had a much better understanding of Jerralee's strange behavior. "I get it now. Her superstitious mind has decided that our love is the result of magic."

"That is true," Zareh pronounced gravely.

"What? You told me you had cast no spells."

"Spells did not bring you together. Only the magic of a perfect love."

Nic groaned. "Now all I have to do is convince her of that. If I can find her."

"I might be able to divine the location of Tiboy's old shack."

Nic scowled and cautioned her against using supernatural means to do so.

"*Non,*" she demurred with a meaningful look. "I was born in the swamp. I know everyt'ing that goes on there."

After a moment Nic smiled with understanding. There was nothing supernatural about Zareh. The powers she possessed were perceptiveness, acute observation and keen native wit. That and a basically credible personality. For the first time in his life, he saw his old friend as she really was.

Zareh's greatest skill was her innate understanding of human nature. People believed in her because she made herself so believable. Her charms worked because those who asked for them expected them to work.

"You're a lovable fake, Zareh." Nic hugged the tall woman fiercely.

She seemed affronted by the accusation, but the smile twinkled. "I am what I am."

"Tell me how to get to the shack."

"You will need a boat. Come, I will draw you a map."

Despite the late afternoon shadows Nic maneuvered his borrowed skiff deftly. If Zareh's map was correct, he would find the old shack just around the next bend. He ducked to avoid a low-hanging swag of moss and when he straightened up he saw a small, weather-beaten structure on the opposite bank.

The building was no more than twenty feet by twenty feet and was constructed of a jumble of different materials. It listed to the leeward side and appeared to be defying gravity. Jerralee's old pirogue was tied to a short pier that extended over the water in front of the shack.

He ran the little motorboat right up onto the bank and cut off the motor. He stepped out of the boat and looked around. Where was Jerralee? She must have heard his approach. Was she planning to try and avoid him way out here as well?

Nic hurried to the little cabin and pounded forcefully on the door. "Open up in there!"

"Go away, Nic."

"I'm not leaving until we get a few things ironed out, so you might as well let me in."

Jerralee rested her forehead against the rough planks of the door. She wanted nothing more than to let him in. She wished with all her heart that he could explain everything away. "There's nothing to talk about."

"I love you, Jerralee. I'm miserable without you."

"Then tell Zareh to put an end to the spell."

"This has nothing to do with Zareh and magic spells."

"It does! She told me herself that she was responsible for bringing us together."

Nic groaned. Would she understand about the IOU if he told her the truth? More importantly, would she be able to forgive?

"She schemed to get us together, but the only magic involved was the magic we made ourselves. I love you, Jerralee."

She flung open the door, but Nic's relief was short-lived. She rushed out of the cabin ready to do battle. "And just how do you explain that?"

"Well, I'm not sure."

"See!" She folded her arms across her chest.

"No, I don't understand."

"This thing between us in not your normal everyday run-of-the-mill variety of love."

"Exactly," he agreed, reaching for her.

She sidestepped and held up her palms to warn him off. "Please don't touch me, that only strengthens the spell."

"You don't believe that."

"I'm so confused, I don't know what to believe anymore," she admitted.

"You are entirely too superstitious."

"It's hard not to be when I've grown up around here," she argued.

"Just forget all that for a few minutes and listen to reason," he yelled.

"Why are you so intense?" she asked.

He laughed. "I think I have a right to be intense. I love you and you love me, but I'm afraid you're going to let some silly superstitions ruin it all forever."

"It's just a spell," she argued.

"It's not a spell. It was meant to be."

"Then how come we didn't get together before now? How could we have kept our distance all these years if it was really meant to be?"

"Maybe we weren't ready before, I don't know. But one thing I do know is that we are in love now. Doesn't that count for anything?"

"It isn't love we're in, it's magic," she insisted.

"You've got me there. This might be magic, but it isn't voodoo! Zareh has assured me of that."

"And you believe her?"

"She's never lied to me. Poets have been writing about the magic of love for centuries."

Jerralee stared at the boggy ground, unable to speak around the lump in her throat. With all her heart she wanted to believe him. But she was too hurt by the other piece of information Zareh had divulged. She didn't know if she could ever forgive Nic for making her fall in love with him just to continue the Delarue line.

Nic tentatively put his hands at her waist. "Don't shut me out, Jerralee. I love you, and I want to spend the rest of my life with you."

She turned the full force of her gaze on him. "How do you feel about children, Nic?"

Although surprised by the question, Nic didn't miss a beat. "I adore them. And you?"

Jerralee jerked herself from his grasp. "That's what this all boils down to, isn't it?" she claimed hotly. "You need to marry a LeBeau to end the curse and ensure the precious Delarue name!"

"That's not true."

"According to Zareh it is. She said she's responsible for getting us together."

Nic sighed. He had hoped he wouldn't have to confess everything at once. "There was no spell cast. All Zareh did was make up that IOU and plant it among your papers. All of which was done with the best of intentions."

"The IOU is phony?" Jerralee had a hard time taking that in. "Why did you insist on paying?"

"I care about you, and I want you to be happy. I felt my family owed it to yours after what happened so long ago," he said earnestly.

It took several seconds for the information to penetrate her foggy brain and then she began questioning Nic's motives all over again. "I don't believe you. You were willing to marry me to reverse the Delarue curse. What else were you hoping to gain?"

"You."

"Got any swamp land you want to sell me?" she asked bitterly.

"That isn't fair."

"For years your lawyers have badgered us to sell the Sweetwood homeplace. I never thought you'd go to such lengths to possess the last piece of LeBeau property."

"You're wrong, Jerralee. Very wrong."

"Maybe, but I could have sworn all those offers to buy had the name Delarue on them."

"I wanted to take that eyesore off your hands as a gesture of goodwill because I knew your family could use the money."

"Philanthropy doesn't become you, Nic." She whirled away and paced along the path in front of the shack.

"I don't know how you can call three offers badgering. If you recall, the first came when I heard you were going to college. I thought you might need the money for your education. The second was right after you came home without your degree. I thought you might need the money to help get your business started. The last time was when your Tante Olivette had surgery."

"When opportunity knocks," she said sarcastically.

"You're being irrational. How can I explain anything to you when you refuse to listen to reason?"

"You can't. I want you to leave, Nic."

"I'm not going until we get this settled."

"Very well then, I'll go." Jerralee stomped all the way to the water's edge.

Nic followed and grasped her arm. "You're not leaving."

"Yes, I am," she cried, jerking her arm free and jumping into the pirogue. "I'm getting as far away from you as I can." She had to because she felt her resistance weakening.

"We're going to talk this out until we get it resolved and I don't care if it takes the rest of our lives." He grabbed her around the waist to haul her back onto solid ground, but she fought his efforts. He finally managed to get her out of her boat and went in up to his knees in the brackish water.

"Put me down!" Jerralee insisted.

"Gladly," he said, suddenly tired of the struggle.

Nic let go so quickly that Jerralee lost her footing and sat down hard in the shallow water. Her eyes widened at the insult and she scooped up a handful of the muddy silt. Using her best pitching skills, she let it fly. The gooey mudball hit Nic's shirtfront with an awful splat.

He roared and Jerralee scrambled to her feet, putting his skiff between them. He was about to give chase when an alligator rose up out of the water near his feet. The animal's great jaws stretched open, then closed with a menacing snap. Its big, empty eyes watched him with a concentration he found highly disturbing.

"Gators," Nic exclaimed quietly. His first thought was for Jerralee's safety. "Get in the motorboat, *cher.*"

She complied, knowing she should tell the truth about this particular gator. In the end, she decided to let him sweat it out a little longer. "What should I do now, Nic?" she asked in a helpless-heroine voice.

He started moving toward the boat. Hoping to divert the alligator's attention, he told her to start the engine.

She gunned the motor and it roared away from the bank in reverse.

"What the hell?" Nic suddenly forgot all about the alligator. "Are you just going to leave me here like this?"

"Yes," she called back. "But I'm taking my gator with me." She gave a high-pitched whistle. "Come on, Crevi, leave the mean man alone."

The giant reptile flopped around as the skiff sped away. He watched it disappear from sight with Crevi paddling in its wake. Nic sloshed up the bank and plopped down on solid ground. The shadows were gloomy among the cypress trees and he knew he would need daylight to find his way out of this unfamiliar area of the swamp. He wasn't going anywhere. Even if he followed Jerralee, there was no way a man in a pirogue powered with a poling stick could possibly hope to catch up with a motorboat.

Frustrated that once again Jerralee's stubbornness had gotten the best of him, Nic went inside the little cabin to await the end of the long, lonely night.

Chapter Eleven

Lively Cajun music filled the night, but its carefree rhythms didn't touch Jerralee. Colorful Chinese lanterns decorated the backyard of Tante Olivette's house, but they did not lighten her gloomy heart. Her young cousin's engagement party was in full swing, and all the members of the extended LeBeau family were having a good time.

Everyone except Jerralee.

She sat in the shadows and moped, hoping no one would notice her. No such luck.

"Minette," Tante Olivette cajoled. "You are not dancing."

"No," Jerralee agreed. "I'm watching Deidre and her fiancé dance. I've never seen her happier."

"She has reason to be happy. She will be a bride soon." Olivette turned back to her niece. "You, Minette, do not look so happy."

"I'm fine." Jerralee's bright smile was false. It was quite a chore to be cheerful when she was so sad. She was beginning to run out of steam. The happiness of others made her feel sorry for herself, and all she really wanted to do was cry.

A local band had been hired for the occasion and when they took a much-deserved break a hundred people groaned their protests. Cousin Hercule stepped up on the front porch and picked up the banjo. Nonc Albert joined in with his harmonica and Cousin Ti'Dan displayed considerable talent on the accordion. After a few moments of errant notes, they struck up a spirited waltz.

The tune made Jerralee recall the day Nic had taken her to lunch in Baton Rouge. He'd held her in his arms and they'd danced to the same song.

She was deep in reverie when his hand touched her shoulder. She knew it was Nic's hand for no other's touch had such power over her senses. She took a moment to steel herself and then glanced around indifferently as if his nearness meant nothing to her.

"I believe they're playing our song," he said with a smile.

She swallowed, trying in vain to dislodge the lump that had suddenly formed in her throat. Nic was the ultimate Southern gentleman in a white planter's suit and blue silk shirt. He had no right to show up at a family gathering looking so drop-dead handsome.

"We don't have a song," she finally managed.

Tante Olivette, who had beamed with pleasure from the moment Nic had appeared, scolded. "Don't be ungracious, Minette. Dance with the man."

"If you knew what he'd done to me, you wouldn't be so eager to send me into his arms."

Ever loyal, Tante Olivette questioned Nic in a no-nonsense tone. "What have you done to my niece, young man?"

"I think we should ask Mr. Delarue to leave." Jerralee stood beside her aunt. "If he refuses, I think we should call the sheriff and have him forcibly removed from the premises."

Tante Olivette ignored this last comment and spoke directly to Nic. "Well, what have you done?"

Nic smiled his most charming smile. "I proposed to her. But my biggest offense was to make her admit she loves me."

Tante shrugged. "That does not sound so terrible, Minette."

"This is ridiculous!" Jerralee shouted, and all heads turned in their direction, but she no longer cared about family opinion. "Let a man offer marriage and it wipes the slate clean. Never mind the circumstances."

The impromptu band was too curious to continue playing and they put down their instruments. They gathered closer and Hercule stepped forward. "What's going on?"

"M'sieu Nic has asked Minette to marry him," Tante Olivette relayed to him and anyone else who might not have heard the news the first time.

Nonc Albert offered his hand. "May I be the first to offer my congratulations."

"No, you may not." Jerralee slapped Nic's hand away. "I wouldn't marry this conniving...Delarue, if he was the last man in the parish."

"Now, now, don't be so hasty, dear girl. Let's hear what the young man has to say in his defense," Nonc Albert said soothingly. Turning to Nic he added, "You do have something to say for yourself, do you not?"

Nic nodded. "I have plenty to say to Jerralee, but I think it should be said in private."

Jerralee propped her hands on her hips. "I have no secrets from my family. Go ahead and explain away. Tell them the only reason you want to marry me is so you can get your hands on the last piece of LeBeau property that's worth anything."

Tante and several others gasped their outrage.

"The only reason I tried to purchase that rotting pile of lumber was because I knew what a financial drain it was for your family to keep it up."

"That's true," Hercule stated. "And he did pay up on that IOU posthaste. Legally, he could have delayed for years."

"There's another example of his scheming ways," Jerralee pronounced. "That IOU was a fake. His housekeeper made it up and planted it among our papers."

"But if the IOU was phony and he knew it, why would he pay it?" Tante Olivette wanted to know.

"Because he was trying to win my trust by hook or by crook," Jerralee pointed out.

Nic laughed ruefully. "I had a perfectly good reason for doing that."

"I'm sure you did. But I don't intend to listen to any more of your excuses." Jerralee turned her back on him. "You've all been fooled, as have I. When was the last time a Delarue ever did anything for a LeBeau?"

"I find it hard to believe, Minette, that you don't know." Tante Olivette shook her head sadly. "I can remember many occasions when one relative or another was in trouble and it was Nic Delarue who came to their aid."

Cousin Beatrix stepped forward. "M'sieu Nic kindly loaned me the money for little Elodie's braces. He allows me to repay him what I can, when I can."

Uncle Ovid spoke up next. "When my boy Jon got in trouble in Baton Rouge, it was Delarue who sent his own lawyer up there to keep him out of jail. He even gave Jon a job at his mill."

Tante Zu would have spoken, but Jerralee interrupted her. "Don't you see what he's doing? Those loans only make us more beholden than we already are."

Nic stood by, silent and stoic. She was desperately fighting against her love for him, so he forgave her for the wounding words. Soon she would run out of lame excuses to keep them apart, and he intended to be there when she did.

"*Non,*" Tante Olivette replied. "They only make us more grateful for the good life we have here and for good friends. LeBeaus do not accept charity."

"The past isn't important," Nic declared. He gazed into Jerralee's eyes and tried to convey all the things he was feeling. "What matters is the future, and how we feel about each other."

Looking love right in the eye and denying it was the hardest thing Jerralee had ever done, but she tried valiantly. "You can't say you don't want me to have your children, can you?"

"No," he said softly. "Of that I am guilty."

"There are worse things, dear girl," Tante Olivette observed.

"You're all a bunch of traitors!" With that Jerralee stomped away.

As though finally remembering why they were having the party, Tante Olivette ordered the band to resume playing. She took Nic's arm and ushered him over to the refreshment table.

"How about something cool to drink?" she asked.

"Now that I've managed to spoil the party, maybe I should just tuck my tail between my legs and slink out of here like the dirty dog I am," he said with an unhappy laugh.

Tante shoved a cold can of beer into his hand. "Not until you've given that pepper-headed niece of mine time to cool off."

He took a long swallow and searched for Jerralee in the crowd. He finally spotted her standing beneath a massive magnolia tree, glaring at him. "I don't know if I have that many years left," he replied.

Looking around, Jerralee spied Richard, the young man from the service station with whom her aunt had once fixed her up. Brazenly, she walked up to him and grabbed his arm.

"Come dance with me," she said. When it looked as if he might refuse, Jerralee flung her arms around his neck.

Nic slammed his can of beer onto the nearby table and stalked off with new determination. When he found Hercule, he dragged him over to where the couple was dancing.

Looking relieved when Nic cut in, the young man quickly disappeared into the crowd.

"Why did you do that?" Jerralee demanded.

"Since you won't talk marriage I think we should conduct a little business. That subject seems to be your primary concern."

"I'll have no more dealings with Delarues. Monday morning I will repay the money for the IOU. At least what hasn't already been spent. The rest I'll repay in monthly installments until I am forever out of your debt."

"Now, wait a minute," Hercule interjected.

"I don't want the money back." Nic was determined to settle things. "In fact, I'd like to right the wrong that was done to your family by mine all those years ago. I'm willing to give you back all the land, one hundred and twenty acres I believe, that is rightfully yours."

"No!"

"Why not?" The shrewd business man in Hercule was aghast at Jerralee's refusal.

"I thought that was the biggest crime against me," Nic complained. "I want to wipe the slate clean."

"No," Jerralee repeated firmly. "That would be charity, and LeBeaus don't accept charity."

"Then I will donate thirty acres and a lump sum of cash to the guild."

"What's the catch?" she asked warily.

"I want a seat on the board of directors."

"Dream on, Delarue," she refused flatly.

"Now hold on a minute, Cousin." Hercule pursed his lips thoughtfully. "I'd advise you to put the matter to a vote. That's the family way."

"Oh, all right." All was lost and she knew it. The family had accepted Nic, and there was nothing she could do about it. He'd earned their friendship and their loyalty, and those things would be his forever.

"I'll get the elders together," Hercule offered, leaving them alone amid the sea of dancers.

"Will you dance with me, *cher?*" Nic asked, holding out his hand, willing her to take it.

She stared at a point over his shoulder and ignored him. But it was hard to ignore Nic and she felt her gaze drawn back to him.

Nic dropped down on one knee in a pleading stance. "Just one dance and then I'll leave you in peace."

The couples surrounding them paused in anticipation of her response. Even the band stopped playing.

"You're making a fool of yourself and of me. Get up," she admonished under her breath.

"I don't care. I'll only get up if you agree to dance with me."

"What good would that do?" she demanded. "Are you so sure of yourself? Is your ego so inflated that you think I'll simply melt into your arms and consent to anything you ask?"

"I can only hope," he answered with outstretched arms.

Jerralee sighed at the futility of resistance. Nic was right. This thing was bigger than the both of them. Emotion clouded her eyes as she stepped into his embrace. They waltzed around the yard to the sentimental Cajun music that swelled up around them. Friends and relatives smiled at the couple and exchanged knowing looks.

As Cousin Beatrix and her husband sailed by, Jerralee heard her say, "Nic Delarue is a good man. Haven't we always known that?"

To which her husband replied, "At last, Minette has found a husband who can control her. And just in the nick of time, too."

Jerralee had almost felt her anger slip away, but when she heard that, it came rushing back. She jerked away from Nic.

"Stop the music," she yelled. "I've had enough. I won't allow my own family to pressure me into marriage because they don't want an old maid in the family. And I refuse to marry any man just so he can put an end to the Delarue curse."

Hercule pushed his way through the crowd to Jerralee's side. "I'd hardly call Nic Delarue, *any man.* He is the man who loves you, Cousin."

Tante Olivette added, "Everyone can see that but you, Minette."

There was a murmur of agreement among the rank and file. Then Olivette continued. "The family is weary of the feud. One hundred years is long enough to carry a foolish grudge, especially when it is so groundless. If Grandfather Jules hadn't been such a fool for drink, he never would've lost the land in the first place. And if he hadn't been such a poor loser there never would've been a Delarue curse."

Hercule spoke up again. "But since there is a curse, and if the only way to end it is for a Delarue to marry a LeBeau, then what are you waiting for, Cousin?"

Jerralee didn't have a chance to answer before Tante Olivette added logically, "Where else are you likely to find a man so willing to marry such a stubborn, hardheaded woman as you?"

The assembly shouted its agreement.

Nic read the uncertainty in Jerralee's eyes and reached for her again. He pulled her close and hoped that he could convey his sincerity. "I love you, Jerralee. I want to marry you, and grow old with you by my side. I don't believe in the curse, and I'm willing to prove it. We don't have to have children, you're enough for me."

Knowing how much he wanted a family, Jerralee realized what a sacrifice he was willing to make for her. In her heart, she knew that he could make such an offer only if his love was true. Secretly celebrating the evidence of his devotion, she felt her doubts begin to dissolve.

She had no intention of letting him make anymore sacrifices. In full view of everyone who was dear to her, Jerralee threw her arms around Nic's neck in a fervent embrace.

"I love you, Nic. I have loved you for a long time, but I wasn't sure about it until now."

"Will you marry me?" he asked again.

"Yes, I'll marry you, and we'll have children."

Applause and hoots of pleasure from the crowd greeted her answer.

Nic grinned and addressed the group. "You all heard her. She can't change her mind now."

"If she does," Hercule pointed out, "you can sue her for breach of promise."

"Cousin!" Jerralee cried. "Is that any way to talk about family?"

"Nic will be family soon, too."

That thought warmed Nic as much as his love for Jerralee. He'd never been part of such a big, happy family before, and the years ahead promised to be interesting indeed.

After much backslapping and congratulatory wishes, Hercule stepped forward. Ever mindful of the future of the craft guild, he immediately made a motion that Nic be awarded a seat on the board of directors. Tante Olivette seconded it and the motion was carried by dozens of happy LeBeaus.

Secure in Nic's loving embrace, Jerralee's "aye" vote was the loudest and happiest of all.

*   *   *   *   *

NORA ROBERTS

Love has a language all its own, and for centuries, flowers have symbolized love's finest expression. Discover the language of flowers—and love—in this romantic collection of 48 favorite books by bestselling author Nora Roberts.

Starting in February 1992, two titles will be available each month at your favorite retail outlet.

In February, look for:

Irish Thoroughbred, Volume #1
The Law Is A Lady, Volume #2

Collect all 48 titles and become fluent in the Language of Love.

LOL 192

THE LANGUAGE of LOVE

Silhouette Romance

LONG, TALL TEXANS

DONAVAN
Diana Palmer

Diana Palmer's bestselling LONG, TALL TEXANS series continues with DONAVAN....

From the moment elegant Fay York walked into the bar on the wrong side of town, rugged Texan Donavan Langley knew she was trouble. But the lovely young innocent awoke a tenderness in him that he'd never known...and a desire to make her a proposal she couldn't refuse....

Don't miss DONAVAN by Diana Palmer, the ninth book in her LONG, TALL TEXANS series. Coming in January...only from Silhouette Romance.

LTT192